THE CHEAPEST NIGHTS

Yusuf Idris

THE CHEAPEST NIGHTS

and Other Stories

Translated from the Arabic
by Wadida Wassef

HEINEMANN
LONDON

THREE CONTINENTS PRESS
WASHINGTON D.C.

Heinemann Educational Books Ltd
48 Charles Street, London W1X 8AH

IBADAN   NAIROBI   LUSAKA
EDINBURGH   MELBOURNE   TORONTO   AUCKLAND
KINGSTON   SINGAPORE   HONG KONG
KUALA LUMPUR   NEW DELHI

ISBN 0 435 90209 1 (AWS)
ISBN 0 435 99412 3 (AA)

First English translation published by Peter Owen 1978
First paperback edition published by Heinemann
  Educational Books 1978

Published in the United States of America 1978
by Three Continents Press
4201 Cathedral Avenue, N.W.
Washington, D.C.

ISBN 0-89410-041-6

UNESCO COLLECTION OF REPRESENTATIVE WORKS
CONTEMPORARY ARAB AUTHORS SERIES

This book has been accepted in the
Contemporary Arab Authors Series of the
Translations Collection of the United Nations
Educational, Scientific and Cultural Organization
(UNESCO).

Set in Intertype Baskerville
Printed Offset Litho and bound in Great Britain by
Cox & Wyman Ltd, London, Fakenham and Reading

Contents

Translator's Note

Although this book bears the same title – *The Cheapest Nights* (*Arkhas Layali*) – as the collection of Idris's stories first published in 1954, the stories herein have been taken, at the author's request, from five other collections as well, in order to represent work from every stage of Idris's development as a writer.

The details are as follows.

From the collection *Arkhas Layali* (1954): 'The Cheapest Nights' (*Arkhas Layali*); 'You Are Everything to Me' (*Abou Sayyed*): 'The Errand' (*Mushwar*); 'Hard Up' (*Shoghlana*); 'The Queue' (*Al Taboor*); 'The Funeral Ceremony' (*Al Ma'tam*).

From the collection *Qua'a Al Madina* (1959): 'All on a Summer's Night' (*Laylat Seif*); 'The Caller in the Night' (*Abou'l Hol*); 'The Dregs of the City' (*Qua'a Al Madina*).

From the collection *Beit Men Lahm* (*A House of Flesh*, 1970): 'Did You Have to Turn on the Light, Li-Li?' (*A Kana La Budd Ya Li-Li An Todi'i Al Noor*).

From the collection *Hadithat Sharaf* (1960): 'Death from Old Age' (*Shaykhookha Bedun Genoon*); 'Bringing in the Bride' (*Tahweed al Aroussa*); 'The Shame' (*Hadithat Sharaf*).

From the collection *Lughat ul Ay Ay* (*The Language of Pain*, 1967): 'Because the Day of Judgement Never Comes' (*Le'anna Al Qiyamata La Taqun*).

From the collection *Akher al Dunya* (*The Ends of the Earth*, 1966): 'The Freak' (*Al Sheikh Sheikha*).

Introduction

Yusuf Idris was born on 19 May, 1927. His father worked on land reclamation projects, a job that required him to be constantly on the move, away from his family and far from city life. Yusuf, his eldest son, was sent at an early age to the country to live with his grandparents. It was a lonely life and the young boy, homesick and estranged, craved affection in a household full of adults and dominated by his grandmother, a dour and undemonstrative woman. He would not have been any happier in his own home, his mother being as stern and intractable as his grandmother. Theirs was a distant relationship with none of the intimate ties that normally bind mother and child. Yusuf missed his father whom he loved, and grew up a solitary and timid boy.

His school was some distance away and on the long walks there and back he learned to take refuge in a dreamworld of his own where his troubles vanished and he was in possession of all the things he missed in reality. At the age of ten his talent was already germinating as he spun himself a whole web of tales which he lived in his imagination.

He returned to live with his parents as an adolescent, joining his two brothers and two sisters. The family moved a good deal from one town in the Delta to another before settling finally in Cairo. It was there that Idris awakened to sex. At the age of fourteen he was having affairs with women frequently twice his age. His main concern then was to vanquish and possess; he was unable to imagine a relationship other than sex binding a man and a woman. It was only later that he felt the need for a deeper tie.

Although he longed for love he feared to give it. In the story 'The Dregs of the City' the hero's restless pursuit of women may well be an echo of the frustrations and secret longings of those days.

Idris decided early in his student career that he wanted to be a doctor, but his years as a medical student were increasingly interrupted by the turbulent political situation in post-war Egypt. He took part in demonstrations against the British and the corrupt system of King Farouk and became executive secretary of the committee for the defence of students. As secretary of the student council he was responsible for revolutionary publications for which he was imprisoned and suspended from college. It was then that he attempted his first short story (1951) which became popular in student circles.

After graduation he was appointed to the Kasr el Eini, Cairo's largest government hospital. His political career continued, however, and he joined underground organizations fighting the British. He supported Nasser's rise to power but, like many others, soon became disillusioned. The clash with Nasser came in 1954 when it became clear that the revolution had accomplished few of its glowing promises. Idris was arrested and interned. During his detention he joined the Communist Party, only to resign in 1956 when he realized he could never accept the totalitarian side of communism.

Yusuf Idris's literary career began when he was a medical student. His short stories started to appear in *Al Masri*, a prominent Cairo newspaper, and in *Rose el Youssef*, a leading weekly magazine. In 1954 his first collection of short stories was published under the title *Arkhas Layali* (*The Cheapest Nights*) with an introduction by the eminent Egyptian writer and scholar Taha Hussein, who hailed him as a young writer of outstanding talent. It was followed by another collection in 1956 which included his first short novel, *A Love Story*. Idris was then still practising medicine, and occupied a post as Health Inspector in the Ministry of Health. The story 'Death from Old Age' is inspired by his experiences there. While continuing to practise as a doctor he briefly took up psychiatry.

In 1960, having decided on a literary career, Idris gave up medicine for good and became editor of the Cairo newspaper *Al Gomhoureya*. Between 1956 and 1960 he had travelled extensively throughout the Arab world, observing new trends and developments. 1961 found him caught up in the Algerian struggle against the French. He joined the rebels in the Algerian mountains and remained there for six months, fighting on their side and later being decorated for valour by the Algerian Government.

On being wounded he returned to Egypt. He was already an established journalist and with the regular publication of his novels, short stories and plays he was soon recognized as one of Egypt's foremost contemporary writers. His short stories were singled out for particular praise, Tewfik El Hakim saying of him that 'Yusuf Idris, in my opinion, is the renovator and genius of the short story.' In 1963 Idris was awarded the Order of the Republic.

Success and recognition did not divert him from political issues. In 1969 he wrote *The Schemers*, a play banned by the censor for being highly critical of Nasser's policies. Nevertheless his short stories and non-political works continued to appear both in Cairo and Beirut, and he kept up his attacks on the existing regime until forced to retire from public view, emerging only after the October war of 1973 when he was appointed one of the literary editors of *Al Ahram*, the leading Cairo newspaper.

In many writings and interviews Yusuf Idris reiterates his conviction that life is a constant process of change with which views and values must keep up. Nothing must remain static. Where there is standstill there is no life. People are not born to accept the situations imposed upon them by previous generations. He is therefore always alert to new concepts and new philosophies. 'In a constantly changing world,' he says, 'a writer is a major factor in revolution.

He has a part to play in society. A writer differs from other people in that he is more impressionable, with a keener sensitivity to his surroundings.' 'When I start writing,' he adds, 'I do not plan ahead. I write from intuition, reflecting the state of man. I have only a general notion in my mind, but I do not know beforehand how the characters are going to behave, or how the story will end. My thoughts are the inspiration of the moment.'

The working class and the struggling poor are Idris's raw material. He depicts them with compassion and understanding. His love and deep attachment to the rural surroundings of his youth show through in many of the stories in this book, especially in 'All on a Summer's Night' where the reader can almost smell the hay and the mixture of odours unique to Egyptian villages. The sufferings and secret dreams of a group of young fellahin are revealed with remarkable sensitivity.

'The Shame' demonstrates Idris's shrewd understanding of the workings of the fellah mind. In 'The Funeral Ceremony' he shows with stark simplicity how the dire struggle for daily bread leaves no room for civilities even in the presence of death. Abdel Kerim in 'The Cheapest Nights' is caught in a dilemma shared by thousands of fellahin all over the country. He is burdened by numerous children. There is nowhere he can go and nothing for him to do on cold winter nights. The meagre entertainments of the village are beyond his means. So he returns to his bed and his wife, to the cheapest pastime, only to father more children whom he cannot afford to feed.

The simplicity of Idris's themes gives vigour to his writing. He passes judgement on no one. He simply brings before us a number of perfectly sketched individuals whose lives he makes us share for as long as the narrative lasts. We see them struggle against their destiny and against the human condition. There is hardly any plot to his stories. He captures the outward behaviour of his characters through a few masterly strokes that reveal their feelings and reactions without resort to psychological analysis. The

ageing policeman afflicted with impotence and torn between despair and humiliation; Abdou who sells his blood
to earn a living; the long-suffering El Shabrawi of 'The
Errand' – all are unforgettable characters revealing Idris's
compassion and his ultimate faith in humanity.

Idris's style is unique in that he is the first writer to have
developed a mode of expression quite new to Arabic literary
tradition by making full use of colloquial Arabic. He makes
a deliberate distinction between the language spoken by
his characters and that which he assumes when he himself
takes over the narrative. This subtle alternation of classical
and spoken Arabic enhances the realism of his work and
his own individuality as a writer. Such a detail will escape
the English reader as the same distinction does not exist
in English. This innovation at first raised an outcry among
Arab critics who saw his work as a deviation from the
tradition and concepts of Arabic literature. They capitu-
lated eventually, however, when it became evident that
the Arab reader, for the first time, was savouring a purely
indigenous product, a stark expression of himself.

Wadida Wassef

The Cheapest Nights

A little after evening prayers a torrent of abuse gushing out of Abdel Kerim came pouring down on the entire village, sweeping Tantawi and all his ancestors in its wake.

No sooner had he rushed through the four prostrations than Abdel Kerim stole out of the mosque and hurried down the narrow lane, apparently irritated, one hand clasping the other tightly behind his back. He was leaning forward, his shoulders bent, almost as if weighed down by the woollen shawl he was wearing, which he had spun with his own hands from the wool of his ewe. Presently he raised his brass-yellow face and caught the wind on the tip of his long hooked nose, blotched with many ugly black spots. He muttered, clenching his teeth, and the taut dry skin of his face wrinkled, bringing the points of his moustache level with the tips of his eyebrows, which were still speckled with drops of water from his ablutions.

His irritation grew as he trudged along down the narrow lane trying to find a path for his large flat feet with cracks in their soles so deep they could easily swallow up a nail.

The lane was teeming with youngsters scattered like breadcrumbs, tumbling about in all directions, and getting in his way. They pulled at his shawl, knocked against him, and made him cut his large protruding toe on the bits of tin they were kicking in his path. All he could do was lash out at them, vituperating furiously against their fathers and their forefathers, the rotten seed that gave them life, and the midwife who brought them to existence. Shaking with rage he cursed, and swore, and snorted, and spat on the wretched town where brats sprouted out of the ground in greater numbers than the hairs on one's head.

But he comforted himself with the thought that the future
was going to take care of them. Half of them were sure to
die of starvation, while cholera would carry off the rest.

He sighed with relief as he emerged from the swarming
lane into the open square surrounding the pond which
stood in the middle of the town. Darkness spread before
him where the low grey houses nestled close to one another,
with heaps of manure piled before them like long-neglected
graves. Only a few lamps shining across the wide circle of
night indicated that there were living creatures packed
beneath their roofs. Their dim red lights, winking in the
distance like the fiery eyes of sprites, came across and sank
in the blackness of the pool.

Abdel Kerim peered into the gloom that stretched before
him, the stink from the swamp winding its way up his
nostrils. It oppressed him so he couldn't breathe. The
thought of the townspeople already snoring behind their
bolted doors oppressed him even more. But now his anger
turned on Tantawi, the watchman, as he recalled the glass
of tea the latter had offered him in the glow of sunset, and
which his parched throat and his longing for it had forced
him to accept at the cost of his pride.

It was very still in the square. Still as a graveyard;
nothing stirred. Abdel Kerim walked on, but half-way
across he halted. Not without reason. Had he followed
where his feet were taking him, in a few paces he would
have been home, and having bolted the door behind him,
there was nothing for him but to flop on his pallet and go to
sleep, and there was not a grain of sleep in his eyes just then.
His head felt clearer than pump water, lighter than pure
honey, and he could have stayed awake till the next crescent
moon of Ramadan appeared. All because he couldn't resist
a glass of black tea, and Tantawi's fiendish smile.

And now he felt no desire to sleep and the townspeople
were all huddled, snoring in their hovels, leaving the night
to their obnoxious children. What was he to do with himself? Stay up. But where? Doing what? Should he join the
boys playing hide-and-seek? Or hang around for the little

girls to gather round him and snigger? Where could he go
with his pockets picked clean? Not a wretched piastre with
which to take himself to Abou El Assaad's den, for instance.
There he could order a coffee and then smoke a water-pipe
and stay till all hours, or sit and watch solicitors' clerks at
their game of cards, and listen to the radio blaring out
things he didn't understand. He could laugh to his heart's
content poking Abou Khalil in the ribs and then move on
to where 'Mo'allem[1] Ammar was sitting with the cattle
dealers and join their conversation about the slump in the
market. But he hadn't a wretched piastre. God bring
your house to ruin, Tantawi!

Nor could he go across to Sheikh Abdel Megid's where
he was sure to find him squatting behind a brazier with a
coffee-pot gently boiling on top. El Sheehy would be there,
sitting near him, telling of the nights that made his hair turn
grey, and the days gone by when he had thrived on the
simple-minded, kind-hearted folks of those days, and how
he was made to repent of swindling and thieving and lay-
ing waste of other people's crops by the wily generation
of today.

No, he couldn't even go there, because only the day
before he had pushed the man into the basin below the
water-wheel and made a laughing stock of him. They'd
been having an argument over the cost of repairing the
wheel. Not a civil word had passed between them since.

If only he could just grab his ferruled cane and go to
collect Sama'an and together make off for the neighbouring farm of El Balabsa. There was fun to be had over
there. Wedding feasts, and dancing girls, and high jinks,
and merry-making, and what-have-you. But where was
the money for all that? Besides, it was late. Very likely
Sama'an would have gone to make it up with his wife
at her uncle's, where she was staying. And the road was
treacherous, and everything was pitch black. Merciful
God! Why must he be the only clod in town tormented

[1] Master of a trade.

by lack of sleep? And Tantawi. *He* wasn't tormented. *He* was probably snoring away peacefully in some quiet nook. God in heaven, let him snore his way to hell!

Suppose now that he were simply to go home like a God-fearing man. He would nudge his wife and make her get up and light the petrol lamp, heat the oven, warm him a loaf of bread and bring him the green peppers left over from lunch. With luck there might be a piece of pie left over too, which his wife's mother had sent them in the morning. And then she'd make him a nice brew of fenugreek and after that, pleased as a sultan, he'd sit and repair the handles of his three worn reed baskets.

Yes, what if he did just that? Would the station take wings and fly, or would the heavens collapse on the threshing floor? He knew no such thing was likely to occur. He also knew his wife. She would be lying like a bag of maize with her brood of six scattered round her like a litter of puppies. Nothing would make her stir. Not even the angel Israfil blowing his trumpet to raise the dead. And even if by some miracle she were to wake up, what then? He wasn't kidding himself. The petrol lamp was only half full and the woman would be needing it when she sat up to bake all night tomorrow. That is, if they all lived till tomorrow. And the children, growing hungry at sundown, would have devoured the last of the peppers with the last scrap of bread. And the pie was sure to have followed after the peppers and the bread. As for fenugreek and sugar, he needn't worry. There simply wasn't any in his house. And never again was he going to be offered a glass of tea like the one he had drained at Tantawi's.

God damn your soul to hell, Tantawi, son of Zebeida!

Anyone coming to relieve himself in the square at that hour, and seeing Abdel Kerim planted in the middle of it like a scarecrow, would have thought him touched in the head or possessed of a devil. He was neither. Just a man whose perplexity was greater than he could deal with.

A simple man, unfamiliar with the things of the night, the tea playing havoc with his head; his pockets stripped clean on a cold winter's night, and all his companions long sunk in deep sleep. What was there for him to do?

He stood thinking for a long time before he made up his mind. Having no choice he crossed to the other end of the square. He could only do what he always did on cold winter nights.

Finally he was home. He bolted the door and picked his way carefully in the dark over the bodies of his sleeping children, to the top of the mud oven. Inwardly he reproached the fates which had plagued him with six bellies so voracious they could gobble up bricks.

He knew his way in the dark from long habit on cold winter nights. And when he found his woman he didn't nudge her. He took her hand and began to crack her knuckles one by one, and to rub against her feet, caked with tons of dirt. He tickled her roughly, sending a shiver down her sleeping bulk. The woman stirred with the last curse he called on Tantawi's head. She heaved herself over and asked nonchalantly through a large yawn what the man had done to deserve being cursed in the middle of the night. Abdel Kerim muttered, cursing whoever drove him to do this, as he fumbled with his clothes preparing for what was about to be.

Months later the women came to him once again to announce the birth of a son. His seventh. He condoled with himself over this belated arrival. All the bricks of the earth would never fill up this one either.

And months and years later, Abdel Kerim was still stumbling on swarms of brats littering the lanes, tumbling about in all directions and getting in his way as he came and went. And every night, with his hands behind his back, catching the wind on his long hooked nose, he still wondered what pit in heaven or earth kept throwing them up.

You Are Everything to Me

All was quiet. The only sound came from the primus stove like the persistent wailing of a sickly child. It was interrupted at intervals by the noise of the metal tumbler dragging on the tile floor of the bathroom, then the sound of water gurgling out of it, and the crackling of the tin can where the water boiled. The sounds clashed and darted about like bats under the low ceiling of the room until at last the primus gave a last gasp and was silent.

It was a long time before the bathroom door opened and Ramadan heard his wife clatter in on her wooden clogs, her familiar breathing pervading the room. The clogs kept clattering up and down and the light from the lamp flickered as the sad low murmur of the woman rose and fell. Ramadan kept his eyes shut. He opened them only when he felt drops of water splash on his face. He stiffened a little at the sight of his wife standing dishevelled with the wooden comb in her hand. She was digging it into her kinky hair, making long deep furrows as she pulled. Her plump face was puckered and there were wrinkles on the sides of her flat nose. She worked at the thick coils, the water splashing about in every direction, wetting her clean cotton dress with the huge faded flowers.

'Why don't you take care with that water, woman,' said Ramadan as he shifted on the bed and shut his eyes again. 'You'll break the lamp.'

He paid no attention to what she mumbled but turned over and settled down to sleep. As he pulled the quilt over his shoulder he opened his eyes a little to steal a look at his wife who was just turning off the lamp with a radiant smile on her clean face. The wrinkles had disappeared for the time being. A little tremor ran through Ramadan's body as he snapped his eyes shut. He had long known the meaning of that smile on Thursday nights.[1]

The four-poster shook as the woman climbed up and slipped under the covers. A strong female odour, mingled with that of cheap soap and the cotton nightdress, pervaded the intimate world under the quilt. Ramadan gave a laborious cough which he made long and deliberate.

'What's the matter?' asked his wife in a meek voice. 'You sure Sayyed is not awake?' she added after a while, in a conspiratorial tone. When she got no reply she gave a sigh which she seemed to draw from the inner coils of her soul while the bed posts shook again and she heaved herself over to place herself within the warm radius of his body. The man was breathing quickly and the hot gusts of his breath bore her off to bowers of bliss, crushing her to the marrow. She stretched a hand and touched his moist forehead, then slid it down to his fat neck where the veins stood out.

'Bless you, my dear. God keep and bless you, love,' she said in a voice like the mewing of a hungry cat. Ramadan forced himself to cough again, groaning through his clenched teeth, and the four-poster shook once more as he turned and showed her his back.

That wasn't the first time he had turned his back, or coughed, or groaned through his clenched teeth. He couldn't remember how many months ago his trouble had started. Whether it was before or after the small Bairam.[2] A thick fog veiled the beginning of it all. He had never given the matter a thought, nor did he dream that what had happened that day would lead him to this. Just like his neighbour from next door, the bus-driver, Si Ahmed, who couldn't have known that the fever which had seized

[1] Friday is the Moslem day of rest.
[2] The small Bairam is the three-day feast following the month of Ramadan.

his little girl would end in a procession of mourners filing
into his house.

He had attributed what happened to a chill he had
caught. When the effects of the cold had gone and he
found he was recovering his strength he decided to sleep
with his wife that same night. The prospect cheered him
up, and he went to take his position in the public square
where he was on duty considerably elated, humming the
only tune he knew. Cars stopped as usual at the signal of
his powerful hand in its worn white glove. He stood erect
in his close-fitting uniform, with the brass buttons pulled
tightly over his paunch making it look like a huge water-
melon. The paint shining on his cap failed, however, to
conceal the grime and the signs of long wear. With his
stubby pencil he diligently took the numbers of offending
cars with the confidence of one who has no fear of the
past, the present or the future. He jotted them down
neatly in his clear handwriting of which he was very
proud. The world was fine, and he was on top of it. He
ruled it with his whistle, exalting whom he wished and
humbling whom he wished with merely a sign from his
gloved hand.

As he wrote out his first summons for the day in his
mind he was already romping in the pastures of bliss
that were promised for the coming night, when he intended
to shake off the dullness of that week of illness. But the
cares of the day and the busy flow of traffic which he
controlled from under the rim of his cap took his mind
off the matter for a while and he remembered again only
when he got home. He had thrown his tired body on the
divan and was struggling to pull off his heavy uniform
boots.

'Here, let me,' said his wife as she squatted on the floor
to help him. Her soft hand went round the calf of his leg
and the tip of his shoe dug between her breasts, which
reminded him of the romp he had in mind and he began
to tickle her with his foot while she leaned back and giggled
and pushed him away. Then she rolled on her side, tighten-

ing her grip round his calf. He enjoyed the game and thrilled to the woman's voice as she squealed with pleasure, half of her willing, half of her holding back and all of her tingling with desire.

Though a fog veiled the beginning, Ramadan could remember that night clearly. Every minute he had struggled, soaking in streams of sweat, shutting off his mind to the entire world until he and his wife and the bed were all that existed.

She pushed him from her again and again, and he damned her to hell over and over, and the struggle went on, halting only when the sleeping boy stirred and resuming when he was heard snoring again, as he drooled down the side of his mouth.

He gave up at dawn, and the woman went to sleep, but not he.

That night went and other nights came and every time he renewed the struggle, fighting desperately for his virility until at last he was forced to give up, saying to himself one morning in a voice he hardly recognized as his own:

' "There is no might or power but in God." You're beaten, man. Finished, washed up.'

Often before, he had avoided his wife at breakfast, but that day he wanted her out of his sight altogether. He could have knocked his head against the wall in his misery. It was a strange thing that was happening to him. The painful struggling every time, and the sweating, and the long nights, should have forced him to admit he was no longer a man. But he could not bring himself to do it. He burned with shame and humiliation just as if he were being paraded through the town sitting naked on a donkey, his head heaped with mud. 'You're finished, man; washed up,' he kept repeating to himself as though he were reciting the *ayah*[3] of The Chair against evil spirits.

[3] A verse from the Koran.

He cut himself a big chunk of bread but left it untouched. He got up and stood looking out of the window. Then he spat. A large mouthful which he aimed at the chicken coops on the facing roof-top. He came back and sat down at the eating board, staring at his food without touching it, chewing on his silence until it choked him. Then he got up again and slipped on his clothes, feeling his body dissolve and his limbs melt into nothing as he stole out of the house.

Standing in the middle of the square where cars milled around him and heaven and earth moved and only he stood dazed and fixed in his place, he suddenly realized the triviality of this kingdom that was his. The white gloves bothered him. His cap weighed on his head like a millstone. All day he did not trouble to write down one summons. And why should he? The world could go to hell for all he cared. He wasn't there to put it right. Damn the cars and their drivers and the traffic, and everything to do with the crazy shrieking merry-go-round where he stood.

For the first time in his life he hated the thought of his home and the wretched face of his wife, and he was in no hurry to return to either. He slid his cap down his forehead and loosened his belt as he trudged heavily down the street, the grooves in his face overflowing with despair, wishing some vehicle would knock him down and put an end to his misery. At last he reached the door of the only man in town who was a friend to all. He stood there and knocked, a thing he did not do frequently. Tantawi was not astonished. He let him in and made him welcome, asking many questions about his health and his friends and his relatives and his hometown and who had married and who had died and who was still alive. But when Ramadan said, 'Tantawi, boy, I want a whiff,' Tantawi was astonished.

Ramadan was not in the habit of taking much hashish, but that night he took an overdose to the point that Tantawi thought it best to see him home. Ramadan was

too dazed to refuse or accept, much less take in his
friend's questions about what was troubling him.

As he walked Ramadan wandered far with his mind,
delving deep in time and place until he reached Sekina,
his neighbour, in the old house by the stream, and the
years following his puberty. From time to time he stopped
in his tracks for no reason and Tantawi would tug at him
and he had to walk on, while his mind still rambled.
'Suppose it works, boy. Suppose hash will do the trick,'
he would cry as the sudden thought struck him, and he'd
burst out laughing, stopping in his tracks again.

'By the Prophet, he's gone. Quite stoned,' murmured
Tantawi with pity for his friend.

Ramadan nearly blurted it all out but caught himself
in time and shoved the words back into his dry throat, as
his shoes hit the road once more and Tantawi pulled him
along by the hand.

Hashish didn't work that time, or any other time.

On the nights when he took it he would remain silent,
speaking little, and when he managed to say something it
was as if the words had been sucked out of him like a bad
fluid; an acrid mixture of anger, resentment and mortification. His wife would chatter on in the meantime, even
though he hardly moved a muscle. His duty in the square
became an agony he was forced to swallow slowly, like
the hours he spent there, only half standing. The brisk
salute he usually gave to his superiors deteriorated to a
half-hearted motion he wrenched from himself like a bad
tooth. And all the time he got more and more entangled
in a coil of lies he was forced to tell the doctor in order
to obtain a day or two of leave.

Normally he never went home without something for
his wife. Now she became used to seeing him come with
his hands empty and dangling at his sides as if they didn't
belong to him.

One day he came home to find his wife's mother had

just arrived for a visit. His cool and indifferent greeting made his wife blush, and her vexation reached a peak as the day wore on and his talk with her mother did not go beyond an occasional, 'And how are you?'

Finally, having had enough, the old lady retired to bed after barely going through her evening prayers, moaning and groaning from her rheumatic joints. An hour later he too was stretched out on the straw mat at the foot of the bed together with his wife and son.

He was awakened at dawn when the old lady stumbled on him as she rose to perform her ablutions for the dawn prayer. And while she recited the *Fatihah*,[4] incorrectly as usual, in her rasping voice, he couldn't help asking himself what in all hell she was doing there.

The answer awaited him in the evening when the Hagga[5] cleared her throat as she squatted on the floor and leaned her back to the wall, draping herself in her large white veil. 'Well, son, I shall not hide it from you,' she began.

In actual fact she was hiding from him that her daughter had sent her a letter behind his back and she began to put the matter forward with the cunning of old women. She took heart from his silence and went on to play mother and sister and bosom friend.

'And for every problem there is a solution, son, don't you worry,' she said.

'Problem my foot!' he fumed inwardly. 'Solution my arse!' he raged. 'What business is it of yours? And what brings you here in the first place, you crumped-up old witch?' The curses he sought to pour out but which he was forced to hold back stoked his fury all the more for until that moment his wife had nothing to do with his problem. She existed nowhere in that vast wilderness where he staggered alone. Now it was obviously no longer his concern alone, and God knows who else was in on it too.

---

[4] Opening chapter of the Koran.
[5] Title given to a person who has been on a pilgrimage to Mecca. It is the feminine form of 'Hagg'.

The evening ended with a tremendous conflagration which overturned the eating board and blew out the lamp, and the neighbours heard it crash to the floor as he roared, 'By God, you will not sleep under my roof!'

The Hagga and her daughter were given shelter by the neighbours that night; and by daybreak the train was carrying the mother back to her village alone. And had there been room in her brother's house for her daughter too, she would not have left her behind.

At that same hour Ramadan was stealing out of their lane. When he met Abu Sultan, his greeting was curt and he avoided his eyes, hurrying along, the sooner to get out of sight. It was the same with Abdel Razek, the newspaper boy, and Hagg Mohamed who sold beans, and everyone else he knew or did not know. Every movement betrayed his secret; every word was a calculated jab; in every smile he saw irony. Everybody knew; even the fellow near him clutching at the ceiling-strap in the train : when their eyes met, it was evident that he knew.

He darted to the centre of the square wishing miserably that his body would shrink and disintegrate and vanish out of sight. Standing there in the middle was like being on display in a showcase open to the curious gaze of the crowds whose only wish was to expose him. When he failed to protect himself from their prying looks he vented his fury on the people, dealing out summonses with a heavy hand, muttering obscenities, and dragging more than one victim to the police station on the slightest provocation.

It was a sad man who stood there every day from now on. Glum, unsmiling, his face dark and lined behind the bushy moustache he no longer bothered to trim. His area became one of dread, and he became the scourge of drivers going through. Everyone knew the dark cop with the bushy moustache. His bad temper, his biting tongue and his aversion to women drivers, particularly those crossing his square, were proverbial.

And then there was his wife.

He had worn himself out, fretting about her. Where was she that day he went home and didn't find her? She said she'd gone to Om Hamida's whose brother was Mehanni – that boy who dressed in ironed silk caftans which clung to his thighs, and wore his skull-cap tilted at an angle. What was she doing at Om Hamida's? And the day he caught her looking out of the window with her head uncovered. The bitch. With her head uncovered!

By and by he took to coming home late at night after he became a regular knocker on Tantawi's door. One night, after he had undressed and got into his white *gallabieh*, fixing his woollen cap firmly on his head, he stretched his weary drugged body on the bed while the voices of the day hummed in his ear and Tantawi's talk flickered on his memory. When the humming ceased and Tantawi faded out he realized his wife was still awake, sobbing bitterly. Ramadan that night had reached the end of his tether. The solid barrier he had placed between them was slowly eroding with her tears until only the quilt remained. He lay still, listening in silence, unable to do anything else. Finally he spoke.

'Just tell me, Naima, what is there I can do?' he asked, every fibre in him crying out in pain.

She only buried her head deeper in the pillow and sobbed louder. He shook her gently, with humility, and asked her again. Not that he expected her answer to help him much. He was simply trying somehow to cover up his failure, or at least to get someone to help him find a way out.

He began to look around to see how others in his predicament acted. He consulted the writings of old. He went to the wise and learned, he visited the shrine of every holy man in town, and he ate the pigeons and mangoes provided by Naima out of her own savings. He sucked the acid tops of sugar cane and he swayed to the beat of the tambourine

when a *zar*⁶ was held in his honour. Many times he was up
at dawn in order to throw the charms written for him into
the sea. Obediently he ate the pies his wife baked him,
kneaded with her own blood, and he drank all the potions
the herbalist concocted specially for him.

Nothing worked.

Then he made his way to the VD hospital, and there
amongst the rows of patients waiting their turn he met
many others like himself. There was comfort in being with
them. The canvas bag which Naima had sewn was filled
and refilled with bottles of medicine which he dutifully
swallowed. His veins and muscles were pricked with hypo-
dermics, and he was admitted for treatment and dis-
charged. His mother-in-law paid them another call, and
the money she brought was spent and much more besides.
Night and day she kept on pouring out advice, and so did
relatives and the relatives of relatives.

Ramadan went on desperately in pursuit of his lost
virility, looking everywhere, following every lead. All his
thoughts, all his actions centred on that one goal. It was
his sole topic : at prayers on Friday, and at the café; at
the fish market and the railway station; with the male
nurse from the hospital and even with his commanding
officer; and still nothing changed.

They were talking quietly one day, Ramadan and Naima,
sitting lazily in a spot of sunshine on the roof. Conversation
flowed gently; Ramadan was relaxing on his day off, and
Naima, having bought the sardines for lunch early that
morning, had given herself up to the luxury of doing
nothing. Ramadan was speaking in the gentlest tone for
he had been giving a good deal of thought to his wife,
and he was blaming himself for much of what was on his
mind. He had chosen that day and that hour to unburden
himself.

⁶ Ceremony for casting out devils.

'Listen, Naima,' he began. He hesitated for an instant then gathered up his courage and went on.

'I . . . I want to do what's right in the sight of God.'

She looked at him languidly. The shadow of a smile, playing on her face, was about to break at his stumbling speech.

'I . . . I think it would be better if I divorced you, Naima,' he blurted out at last.

At this she sat up sharply and turned to face him. She beat her breast with her hand and looked at him with eyes full of reproach.

'Ramadan! For shame! What is this you're saying! You are everything to me,' she exclaimed with indignation, 'father and brother; the crown upon my head. I am not worth the ground under your feet. I am only your servant, my love. How could you say such a thing! After my hair's turned grey, and yours too. . . . It's not as if we're young any more . . . how could you . . .' A gush of tears stopped the words in her mouth and she couldn't continue. She unfastened her head-kerchief and wiped her tears with it as she got up and stumbled downstairs, leaving Ramadan behind, absently passing his fingers over the wrinkles on his face. He smoothed his balding head and passed his hands across his bloated belly. Absently he plucked at the hairs of his leg, most of them turned white, as his eyes strayed to Sayyed, his son.

He gazed at the boy as if he had just discovered him.

Sayyed was lying near him, his face covered with his arithmetic copybook. Wide-eyed and incredulous Ramadan was devouring the boy with his eyes. God almighty! How could he forget Sayyed in his mad pursuit of his virility! How could he forget he had a son, and think only of himself in this whole wide world?

'Sayyed . . . Sayyed, my boy, come over here,' he whispered hoarsely. 'Come, sit here by me . . . let me look at you. My, but you've grown, son. You're almost as big as I am. You'll be a man, soon . . . a man! And I'll have you married . . . that's right, I'll have you married to a beautiful girl. No . . . four! Four beautiful girls, and you'll be their man, son. Do you understand? Do you understand what it means to be their man? Never mind. You will, you will. And you'll have children. Do you hear? You'll have children, Sayyed, and I'll carry your little ones in my arms. These arms of mine . . . do you hear me, son . . .?'

The Errand

Whenever anyone mentioned Cairo in his presence El Shabrawi got terribly upset. It made him feel cheated of his life and he would suddenly long to go back if only to spend one hour at El Kobessi or Mo'allem Ahmed's in the quarter of El Tourgouman. His memory took him back to the days when he was a conscript and he used to go the length and breadth of Cairo every week, and he would hanker for one of those daytime shows he used to attend at the National Cinema. He sighed bitterly every time, for it was not too much to ask God to arrange for the proper circumstances and a little money to make his wish come true. 'I'll give my life for one hour in Cairo,' he never tired of saying.

But he didn't have to go to quite that extreme for things looked up unexpectedly, all of a sudden, and his wish came to be realized in a way he least suspected. One day as he was sitting in his usual place at the police station, as he had for the past four years, a large crowd of people suddenly came barging in. After many questions and in spite of the racket, he was able to make out that they were bringing in a mad woman from Kafr Goma'a accompanied by her relatives and friends. Everyone was yelling at once as more and more people kept coming in, attracted by the noise, until the place was in an uproar.

A beam of hope made his heart flutter. Obviously the woman would have to be sent to the asylum in Cairo with a special escort, and he couldn't think of anyone better qualified for the task than himself.

He found it no problem to get the job. There was no need to send mediators to plead with the adjutant, since all his colleagues bluntly refused to have anything to do with it, and when he volunteered of his own free will there were no objections and the matter was settled right away.

Immediately he dispatched Antar, the errand boy from the station canteen, to inform his wife he was going away. She was to send him some food wrapped in his large handkerchief and the fifty-piastre note she would find hidden in the pillowcase.

In half an hour everything was ready : the Health Inspector's report written and the railway ticket-forms filled. All he had to do was board the train and he would be in the heart of Cairo.

He could hardly believe his luck. He couldn't believe he was going to see Cairo again and go on a tram ride and meet his old friends and dine on grilled meat at Mo'allem Hanafi's. His joy knew no bounds as he walked resolutely to the station at the head of more than a hundred people all recommending that he be kind and patient with Zebeida.

He was given a twenty-piastre tip by her father, and ten by her husband. He shook his head many times and kept up a broad smile and told everyone not to worry. He was going to be like a true brother to her, born of her own mother and father.

It was a strange procession running through the town, with El Shabrawi at the head. People stopped to stare. Those who knew him asked where he was going.

'Only round the corner,' he replied with modesty.

'How far?' they persisted.

'Oh, only up to Cairo,' he said with feigned indifference. 'Lucky man!'

His belly tingled with excitement.

After a long wait the Delta train came puffing in. He got on with Zebeida who sat down quietly beside him. Presently the train started. El Shabrawi felt for his papers for the third time. They were safe in his inside pocket. Seeing all was well and everything in order, he removed his wide

uniform belt and relaxed, sitting back a little, almost forgetting Zebeida.

After a long time the loitering and meandering and
interminable stops came to an end and the train crawled
into Mansourah like a long caterpillar. When they got off
El Shabrawi crossed the bridge holding Zebeida by the
hand, all the time invoking the blessings of the Sayyeda
Zeinab.[1]

He looked for the train to Cairo and found it crouching
in its place, waiting for him. He got on and sat Zebeida
near the window. When the lemonade man came round
he bought two glasses which he gulped down one after
the other. Then he bought a third one which he offered
to Zebeida who rejected it irritably. He patted her sooth-
ingly on her back and gulped it down himself.

The train began to move. The passengers were sitting
snugly in their seats, idly staring at nothing. Zebeida was
looking out of the window like a child, a beatific smile on
her face, while El Shabrawi lost himself in visions of
approaching bliss.

Just before they reached Simbellawen Zebeida suddenly
turned round and beat her breast violently, looking at El
Shabrawi in a strangely accusing manner. The latter
snapped out of his visions with a jolt.

'What . . . what's the matter?' he asked anxiously.

She gave no reply but, holding her hand above her
mouth, let out a joyful trilling-cry which she followed by
a string of others. A sudden hush fell on the carriage and
the passengers all turned to stare. El Shabrawi's head reeled
with embarrassment as he fumbled for an explanation. He
tried to swallow but his throat felt dry. He turned to
Zebeida and implored her to stop, gently patting her hand.

'There, there, now, don't worry, everything will be
alright. Please. . . .'

Finally she calmed down. But the passengers did not.
They began to comment on what had just happened in

[1] Granddaughter of the Prophet.

low whispers that grew steadily louder, never taking their eyes off Zebeida or El Shabrawi.

'Must be his wife, poor dear,' he heard a woman say.

A peal of laughter rang out at one end of the carriage. The man sitting in front of him woke up and cleared his throat. Two children stood on their seats to get a better view. El Shabrawi broke into a sweat that seeped through his khaki uniform. He felt like changing the bitter taste of his mouth so he opened his large handkerchief in order to spit in it but his throat was too dry and he folded it up again and put it back in his pocket.

'What's wrong with the lady, Officer?' asked his neighbour, who did not seem to appreciate the situation.

'Oh, n . . . nothing,' replied El Shabrawi. He was able to recover his speech though his knees still felt rather watery. 'Just a little . . .', he said making a circular motion with his hand near his temple. The man shook his bulk and nodded knowingly. El Shabrawi was still moving his hand when Zebeida turned on him again.

'What do you mean, nothing? Who said there was nothing?' she asked in a shrill cry.

El Shabrawi looked at her with genuine alarm as she poked her face close to his. He leaned back until his head hit the wall, placing his knotted handkerchief, with its contents, between them. She stopped abruptly and stood up with a jerk. She peered unsteadily at the ceiling and screamed again at the top of her voice. 'Who said there was nothing? Down with the Omdah[2] of our town Ibrahim Abou Sha'alan! . . . Long live His Majesty the King, President Mohamed Bey Abou Batta!' And another trilling-cry went up.

The carriage was now in utter pandemonium. Sleeping passengers woke up. The man sitting in front of El Shabrawi pulled his basket from under his seat and hurried away. In one second Zebeida and El Shabrawi had half the carriage to themselves, while the rest of the passengers

[2] Headman.

huddled apprehensively in the far corner. Some left the
carriage altogether while a few remained out of curiosity.
El Shabrawi's uniform was now drenched in perspiration.
He tried to force her back into her seat but she jerked his
hand away.

'Down with our Omdah!' she shouted again to the tune
of more trilling-cries. 'Long live His Majesty the King,
President Abou Batta!'

Everyone was laughing, even the boys selling peanuts and
soft drinks. El Shabrawi joined in too, seeing no reason
why he shouldn't, but he soon had to stop as the situation
suddenly threatened to take a turn for the worse. Zebeida
was preparing to take off her dress, the only garment she
had on. He made an effort to grab hold of her hands but
she pushed him away, still uttering her piercing cries.
Soon they were caught in a scuffle. He won in the end,
forcing her back into her seat, and tying her down with
a muffler which a passenger lent him – but not before she
had flung his tarboosh out of the window. He was incensed,
for throughout his years of service he had never once been
seen without it, and now he had to suffer the indignity
of remaining with his head uncovered except for his
cropped, scanty hair. With that much accomplished Zebeida
was apparently still not satisfied. She continued her volley
of trilling-cries, and every time it was down with the
Omdah and long live the President.

As the train neared Bilbeiss she was starting to calm
down and some of the bolder passengers were encouraged
to return to their seats. Infuriated by the loss of his tarboosh, it was all El Shabrawi could do to refrain from
throwing her overboard. There was nothing for him but
to simmer in his rage until the train pulled in at Cairo.

He waited until all the passengers got off, then he
caught her arm like a clamp and marched her out. As
they walked down the platform he relaxed his grip a little
when he saw she was following meekly, tame as a lamb.

The imposing structure of the station hall filled him
with awe, but in his present state of mind he was in no

mood to relish his surroundings or to allow happy memories to invade his thoughts. Immediately he boarded a tram, with Zebeida obediently in tow, and got off at Ataba. From there he took a short cut to Al Al Azhar Street where he bought himself a new tarboosh with the twenty piastres her father had given him, cursing Zebeida all the time, together with her father and his illicit money. The new tarboosh bothered him, it weighed a ton.

Taking thought he decided to get rid of Zebeida before he gave himself up to the joys of the capital. So he squeezed with her into another tram. As it wound its long, tortuous way through the crowded streets of Cairo El Shabrawi sat reviewing all the mishaps he had suffered up until now and glumly contemplated those yet to come.

Somewhere in the middle he remembered Zebeida and threw a quick glance in her direction. With her jaw hanging open, a fatuous and placid expression on her face, she was leaning heavily on the man standing next to her. The latter had his eyes on the paper he was pretending to read, but seemed obviously to be enjoying himself. El Shabrawi pulled her away roughly. The placid expression vanished and a nasty look came in its place. Once again the trilling-cry went up, and again it was down with the Omdah and long live President Abou Batta.

The conductor blew his whistle and stopped the car midway between stops. He went up to El Shabrawi and ordered him to take Zebeida and get off, roundly abusing him for exposing the passengers to so dangerous a creature.

Finding himself in the street again El Shabrawi decided it would be wiser to cover the rest of the way to the Governorate building on foot. Zebeida walked alongside on his right, her trilling-cries rending the air. A large crowd was collecting behind them as they walked along, El Shabrawi hardly daring to raise his eyes from the ground in his mortification.

The guard at the door anticipated some sensational happening as he saw the crowd approach. El Shabrawi enquired about the Governorate doctor. The guard's prac-

tised eye took in the situation at a glance. He was very
sorry indeed but it was past six and there was nobody
there. El Shabrawi's heart sank.

'And what do I do now?'

'Come back tomorrow,' the guard returned calmly.

'Tomorrow?'

'Morning,' he specified. He turned and shouted at the
crowd which began to disperse loaded with a stock of
anecdotes.

El Shabrawi begged to be allowed to stay the night.
Having nothing more to add, the guard did not bother to
reply, and knowing better than to argue El Shabrawi
grabbed Zebeida by the hand again and moved away.

Slowly, the enormity of his predicament began to dawn
on him. With Zebeida tied to his neck there was nowhere
he could stay the night. He was tired and worn out and he
had had nothing to eat for hours.

He walked into the nearest café in Bab El Khalq and sat
down, keeping her close by his side, paying no attention
to the many stares that fastened on them. He ordered tea
and a water-pipe and was just starting to give himself up
to the delicious euphoria that was spreading to his tired
limbs when a sudden rumbling in his belly made him
almost double up with pain. He realized he couldn't
wait. He must find the toilet. When he enquired of the
waiter, the latter pointed to a place not too far off. But he
had to park Zebeida somewhere. He took a look round the
place and noticed a man sitting near them who was wearing
a coat on top of his *gallabieh*. It was not difficult to start
a conversation with him. It turned out he was a police
detective and El Shabrawi found himself obliged to tell
him the whole story, asking him in the end if he'd mind
keeping an eye on Zebeida while he went to the loo. No
sooner had the man accepted with reluctance than El
Shabrawi had shot out of sight.

When he got back he found the café had turned into a
fun-fair, with Zebeida as the star attraction. Furiously he
pounced on her and dragged her away with profuse

apologies to the police detective. He walked out blindly with no idea where to go. It was getting dark and the glaring lights of the city dazzled him with memories of those bygone days, sadly overshadowed by all he was having to endure.

Probing his memory he recalled a distant relative, a student of agriculture. His memory threw up the address as well, somewhere in Giza, but when he got there he lost his way as he had only been to the house once before and that was during the daytime. He found it in the end, however, after a long search, and his relative gave him a warm welcome, asking where he'd been all this time and how everybody was. El Shabrawi was just about to open his mouth and explain the purpose of his visit when Zebeida, until now on her best behaviour, sent up one of her choicest trilling-cries. If he had had a knife on him El Shabrawi would gladly have cut her throat. He didn't even try to explain why he was there, but hurriedly took his leave and scuttled away allowing his relative only snatches of the story.

When the streets contained them once more, he dug his fingers fiercely into her arm and longed to crush her bones. The thought of murder occurred to him even though he knew it meant a life sentence. He was past caring. Meanwhile Zebeida was waddling along beside him like a goose, totally impervious to the threats he kept muttering at her between his teeth. Suddenly he had a flash of inspiration as the thought of murder and the life sentence he was prepared to face made him see visions that evoked the police station. He could think of no better place to take shelter that wretched night.

So they got on a bus and a moment later they were standing before the sergeant on duty at the Sayyeda headquarters. Being well-practised by now, it did not take El Shabrawi long to sum up the situation for him. The sergeant shook his head slowly.

'That's a responsibility I will not risk.'

'Take us into custody then,' suggested El Shabrawi, his

rage starting to mount.

'That's still a responsibility,' returned the sergeant indifferently.

As he left the building El Shabrawi was bitterly cursing responsibility and everything to do with it, including himself for having volunteered like a fool to take Zebeida to Cairo. For a moment he considered an hotel but gave up the idea when he remembered he would have to account for Zebeida, plus the fact that it would fleece him of at least fifty or sixty piastres which anyway he didn't have. The Sayyeda Zeinab mosque, which was not far off, seemed to offer the only solution, so he took himself there and, grabbing Zebeida, pulled her down by his side as he sat down on the ground by the wall. He was now on the verge of tears and only his pride kept them back. He could think of no one in the world more miserable than himself at that moment.

The place was swarming with the usual crowd of saintly idiots and half-wits always to be found in profusion around a shrine, so that when Zebeida started up her piercing cries her voice was lost in the din of their mutterings and the chattering of the women and the giddy whirlpools of the rings of *zikhr*.[3] El Shabrawi was glad of that. Something like relief began to ease his torment at last, for now Zebeida was in her element. Nothing she could do was going to appear odd in those surroundings. It was he, rather, who was feeling out of place and he longed to lose his reason too and join these carefree people in their bowers of lunatic bliss.

Slowly, and in spite of himself, he began to relax, forgetting his troubles and his frustrations as he sat watching their antics. They were quite an entertaining lot. They did what they liked and nobody stopped them. He turned his attention to a Sheikh who was lying down near him at the foot of the wall. Leaning his head on his arm, the man was watching the people come and go with perfect

[3] Religious exercise where men stand in a ring chanting the name of God.

detachment, a rapt expression on his face and a look of pure contentment in his eyes. Every now and then he would look down, then up at El Shabrawi, then in a mocking drawl order him to repeat the profession of Allah's unity, fixing on him a relentless stare. El Shabrawi could only comply.

As the Sheikh lay there, his vacuous thoughts dwelling on nothing, a cigarette stub fell at his side. Nonchalantly he picked it up and inhaled deeply, enjoying the smoke with obvious relish. He fixed a rapturous gaze on El Shabrawi as the smoke coiled slowly round his face.

'Say there is but one God,' he ordered again in dead earnest, which made El Shabrawi chuckle in spite of himself. Suddenly he longed to lie down too, brainless and free of care like the Sheikh. That reminded him of Zebeida. He turned to look at her and was overjoyed to see she was beginning to yawn. Little by little her body relaxed, her eyelids drooped and slowly she sank into sleep.

Now for the first time El Shabrawi was able to contemplate her face. She wasn't pretty, but her skin was fair and she was small. Her feet, weighed down by heavy anklets, were covered with bruises and layers of mud. The peaceful mask of her face now totally concealed her insanity. El Shabrawi noticed that her gown was torn and her thigh was showing through. He covered her up and looked away. Then he turned to the Sheikh and engaged in an endless rambling conversation with him until the latter fell asleep.

As the dark and the silence grew, and the saint's followers bundled up and lay snoring by the wall like tired monkeys at the end of a long day, El Shabrawi realized his angry mood had left him. He couldn't recall the exact moment when it had happened; he settled down, resigning himself to the snoring that rose all around him, nearly raising the saint from the dead.

Although it had been a long day and he was worn out by the journey and all he had gone through, he decided to sit up through the night. He could hardly wait for day-

light to come as he dozed fitfully, his eyes never leaving
the big clock in the square.

On the dot of seven he was standing in the Governorate
building waiting for the doctor and shooing away the
crowd that had collected like flies. Zebeida meanwhile
was sustaining a new barrage of trilling-cries. Finally the
doctor arrived, and after many ordeals El Shabrawi and
Zebeida were conducted to his presence. He turned her
papers over and scribbled something.

'Take her to the Kasr el Eini to be put under observation.'

They withdrew, and hopping again from one tram to
another, found their way to Kasr el Eini. There, he stopped
a man for information but got no answer. Another looked
at Zebeida and walked on. Finally an old nurse showed
them the way to the out-patient clinic.

The doctor in charge listened patiently to Zebeida calling for the Omdah's downfall and long life for the President. And he laughed long and heartily as he questioned
her and she ranted in reply. El Shabrawi looked on hope-
fully, beaming with pleasure, seeing they were getting on
so well. But the doctor at last put on a serious expression
and informed them there was no room in the observation
department. He put that in writing on the papers.

'Where do I go now?' asked El Shabrawi, his soul about
to leap from his breast.

'Back to the Governorate.'

'Again?'

'Again.'

The entire globe seemed to weigh on his head as he
walked out of the building. Thoughts of murder returned.
He would kill the lot. Zebeida, the doctors, the lot, and
then he would feign insanity and that would be all. But
it was only a fleeting notion.

He trekked back to the Governorate building and arrived
gasping for breath. The doctor turned the papers over
and asked El Shabrawi if they had brought a relative with
them. His heart sank as he said they hadn't. The doctor

explained that the hospital forms could not be filled out except in the presence of a relative. He must take her back where they came from.

El Shabrawi paled.

'You mean take her back to Dakahlia?'

'That's right.'

Come to think of it, El Shabrawi told himself, perhaps it was just as well. But a sudden thought struck him.

'But that's not possible, my Bey, I have only one return ticket form, for me alone.'

'I told you, one of her relatives must be present.'

'Please, my Bey, I beg of you.'

'That's a responsibility I am not prepared to take.'

El Shabrawi had more than his bellyful of responsibility by now. Just as he was about to give vent to his fury and smash everything in sight, the air was rent by one of Zebeida's choice trilling-cries and in less than a second she had ripped off her threadbare gown and dashed out stark naked into the courtyard while everyone looked on, speechless and immobile.

El Shabrawi was the first to move and he shot after her like a dart. A crowd of policemen and detainees ran to encircle her. El Shabrawi succeeded in holding her down but she wriggled out of his hands, calling for the Omdah's downfall. Then she turned and dug her teeth viciously into his flesh. He cried out in pain and came down harshly with a slap on her face. Blood trickled slowly through her teeth. She was carried back struggling and screaming, wildly shouting her battle-cry, her shrieks piercing the sky.

It took four people to get her into the straitjacket.

She rolled on the ground as she fought to get free, foaming at the mouth, her face scarlet with the streaming blood. The doctor filled out a form in a hurry, and El Shabrawi looked on horrified, his whole being wrung with pity at what Zebeida was doing to herself.

The sight of Zebeida in a straitjacket made him realize for the first time that she was really insane. It was a shock. He realized too that she had no understanding whatever

of the things she was saying, that she was not to be blamed
for what he had gone through, and that she had had
nothing to eat or to drink since they had left their town.
The sight of her rolling and writhing on the ground filled
him with pity.

'Alright,' the doctor was saying.

Now at last Zebeida was off his hands and he was
finally rid of her. When that moment arrived he had
promised himself a feast in celebration. But now he felt
strangely unmoved, as if none of it all had anything to do
with him.

The ambulance arrived and Zebeida was hustled in
calling long life to His Majesty the President, her shrill
cries never relenting, to the delectation of the jeering crowd.

Suddenly El Shabrawi darted forward like one stabbed
in the heart and begged the driver to wait. He ran to the
corner and bought her a loaf of French bread and a piece
of *halva*, which he gave to the policeman escorting her.

'Will you see that she eats them,' he pleaded, 'and will
you take good care of her? Please . . . for the sake of all
your departed loved ones. . . .'

When the car rolled out of sight El Shabrawi stole away
straight to the station. He had had enough of Cairo, and
enough of the whole world. From time to time he'd stare
at the hand that had struck Zebeida and his flesh would
creep with a sense of shame he had never known before
in his life.

Hard Up

Abdou was hard up. Not for the first time. The condition was chronic. He had spent most of his life until now trying to make ends meet.

He had started out as a cook, having learned the trade from Hagg Fayed, the Syrian, and mastered it to the extent that the master himself used to exclaim over the well-seasoned, perfectly-spiced sauces he could make. But then nothing lasts for ever. From being a cook he got himself employed in the workshop next door to the restaurant where he was working. Then he was fired, and he found another job as a door-man looking after a block of flats ten storeys high. When for some reason he quit that too, his enormous frame and strong muscles qualified him to be a porter loading trucks, until he developed a hernia. Besides good muscles he had a good voice, not a particularly pleasing one but powerful enough to bring the whole street to him when he found himself hawking cucumbers and melons and grapes.

At one time he worked as a middleman roaming the alleys night and day, in search of a vacant room. He generally succeeded in finding one, and the ten piastres that went with it. Eventually he worked his way up to the inner circles where he learned how to wangle the ten piastres from his clients without having to roam alleys or necessarily to find a room. As for being a waiter, there was none to compare with him. He remembered how, when he was in his prime, on the eve of a feast, he could handle an entire café single-handed without once delaying an order or breaking a glass.

He had a wife with whom he lived in one room surrounded by many neighbours. The neighbours were decent

people on the whole, if one overlooked the brawls that
erupted periodically between his wife and theirs. They
sympathized with him and lent him money when he was
out of work, and prayed for him to find a job and borrowed from him when he did. And so life went on provid-
ing their daily bread, growing daily more niggardly, it is
true, but then, such was life.

So Abdou was hard up. Only this time it had lasted
longer than usual, and there seemed to be no end in sight.
His feet were worn out from calling on old friends and
acquaintances, and every time he returned home and
knocked on the door with a frown on his face and nothing
in his hands. His wife would not greet him when she
opened the door, nor would he greet her, instead he made
straight for his straw mat and tried to go to sleep, shutting
his ears to Nefissa's incessant chatter. But she would force
him to listen, droning on about the events of the day,
and the landlord's threats, and the scraps of bread the
neighbours sent out of charity, and about the coming feast,
and how much she was yearning for peaches, and their
little girl who had died, and the boy she was expecting
who was going to be born with a peach for a birthmark
because she was yearning so for peaches. And she would
go on and on, getting so carried away that her voice would
grow unbearably shrill, until he could stand it no longer.

Nor could he stand to see the pity in the eyes of his
neighbours who felt sorry for him, or listen to them wishing him better luck, because their wishes were no good to
his empty stomach or to Nefissa's almost naked body.

One day on his return home Nefissa announced that
Tolba had sent for him, which gave him a glimmer of
hope, ungrounded perhaps, but still better than nothing.
So he got up immediately and took himself over to Tolba's.
Tolba was undoubtedly the best tenant in the building
because he worked as a male nurse at the hospital. He
was also the most recent tenant.

Tolba received him with much cordiality which threw
Abdou a little out of countenance. No sooner had they

exchanged the perfunctory words of greeting than Abdou was already telling him all about himself. He loved to dwell on the good old days and tell of the various jobs he had held at at one time, and all the people he had known, particularly when he noticed the revulsion which his worn and threadbare *gallabieh* aroused. He felt somehow that speaking of his days of glory covered up for his shabby dress. He swelled with pride and he felt elated talking of the days when he occupied positions of importance. But when he remembered his present plight he grew dejected again. He deplored the evil in men's hearts, and bemoaned the old days of plenty, his voice tapering to a bare whisper which rose from the abyss of his degradation, asking Tolba in the end if he could find him a job.

Tolba listened, although he interrupted him many times, but told him in the end that there was, in fact, a job waiting for him.

That night Abdou went home in a transport of joy. He spoke at length to Nefissa about Tolba's kind heart, and told her she must go to his wife next day after she'd finished with her washing for the students she was working for, and give her a hand and keep her company.

Next day Abdou was up at the crack of dawn, and by sunrise he and Tolba were standing before the Blood Transfusion Department of the hospital. He waited. Others came and waited too. At ten o'clock the door opened and they all went in. The silence impressed him. The air was permeated with carbolic acid which gave him a slight nausea. They were made to line up and a cross-examination began. They wanted to know his father's name, and his mother's, and they wanted to know what his uncles had died of, paternal and maternal, and they asked for his photograph and he could only produce the one stuck on his identity card which he always carried with him in case of an accident or trouble with the police.

They stuck a needle in his vein and drew out a bottleful of blood and told him to come back next week.

During the week he was still hard up, still searching

for a job and nothing was left of the scraps of bread the
neighbours had sent in charity. On the appointed day of
the following week he was at the hospital department again.
At ten o'clock the door opened. 'Not you,' they said to the
man standing in front of him. The man refused to budge.
'Your blood's no good,' they said to him as they shoved
him out of the way.

Abdou's heart sank, but when his turn came and they
told him they would be taking blood from him his apprehension was gone. He stood obstinately in his place and
cheered and laughed much like his old ways, resigned to
wait although he was feeling very hungry.

Soon his turn came. They put his arm through a hole
just large enough to hold it. He was a little alarmed but
when he saw there were two other men on either side of
him his fears subsided. Suddenly he felt as though his
arm were encased in a block of ice. Something like an
obelisk seemed to penetrate it. He gave a moan and then
he was quiet. Presently he began to take a look at his surroundings. He raised his head a little to look through the
glass partition behind which pretty girls who did not have
crooked and protruding front teeth like his wife's, and
who did not wear dull black dresses like her, moved about
quietly. Peering more closely he realized they were not
all girls. Some were young men with clear shiny faces. He
envied them for being inside with the pretty girls and he
wished that by some freak he could make his arm stretch
and stretch until it reached the mask on the girls' faces and
he could pull it away and pinch one of those lovely cheeks.

Abdou kept watching the masked faces until they started
to blur and fade out, and the glass screen began to send
flashes of light, and the masks kept sliding on and off.
Suddenly he felt very tired. His arm went cold, then hot,
then cold again.

'How much are they taking?' he asked the man on his
right.

'I don't know. Half a litre, they say,' said the man. The
conversation ended there.

'Alright, it's over,' someone said, tapping his arm.

Abdou got up, walking unsteadily. When he asked for the money he was told to wait, so he waited. They gave him one pound and thirty piastres minus tax. They were even so generous as to give him breakfast.

Before going home he called at the butcher's and bought a pound of meat, and at the greengrocer's to buy potatoes, and when he knocked on the door of their room he was all smiles. Nefissa beamed with pleasure and cheerfully returned his greeting when she saw what he was carrying. She was quick to come forward and relieve him of his load, and only coyness kept her from telling him how much she loved him.

Soon she was busy cooking, and the frying smells filled the room and escaped outside to the whole building and reached the neighbours, which made some of them smile and others sigh with pity.

Abdou ate until he could eat no more and on a rash impulse went out and bought a water-melon. That night his wife, for once, did not start up her usual racket. She was docile and meek and they cooed like lovers.

Before the week was out Abdou had spent all the money. On the appointed day he went back to the hospital and stretched out his arm and they took their ration of blood and gave him his ration of money and a meal in addition.

Abdou was quite pleased with his new job as he did not have to take orders from anybody, and no one bullied him around. All he was asked to do was turn up every week at that nice clean place where everything was white, and give half a litre of blood and cash in the price. His wife managed to make do with what he gained, and his body managed to replenish its blood supply, and then he went back at the end of the week and gave them more blood and they gave him more money.

And so it went on. Many people envied him.

As for his wife, it all depended. When he came home with food she'd smile in his face and nearly cry out for joy. But when he slept all week she wouldn't leave him alone. She'd nag about his skinny legs and haggard face, and tell him in no polished terms what the women in the neighbourhood were saying about him. How they threw it in her face that her husband sold his blood for a living. Sometimes she'd fuss about him like a hen, seeing that he was warm enough at night, pulling up his cover if it happened to slip. By day she wouldn't let him move from his place and she'd hover round him answering his every call as if he were a sick child.

All this did not escape Abdou. It made him bitter, but then what did it matter? It's true he felt dizzy every time he gave blood, and he had to lie down by the hospital wall until late afternoon. It was also true that people talked, but at least the stove was going and the rent was paid. People could go to hell.

Except that one day when he went to the hospital as usual they did not put his arm through the hole. Instead they called him and said no.

'Why not?'

'Anaemia.'

'What's anaemia?'

'No red corpuscles.'

'So what?'

'It won't do.'

'And what am I to do?'

'Come back later, when you're stronger.'

'I'm strong now. Here. I can tear down that wall.'

'You'll collapse.'

'Don't worry.'

'You could die.'

'I'll take the risk.'

'That wouldn't be human . . . your own good . . .'

'And is what you're doing human?'

'That's how it is . . .'

'You mean nothing doing?'

'Nothing doing.'

That day they forgot to give him a meal, and Abdou was hard up again.

The Queue

In the countryside all marketplaces look alike, more or less.
They all consist of a large vacant lot with a fence and a
gate. They all have stalls with empty wooden shelves dis-
torted by the heat and the winter cold. Here and there
you will find a few benches made of hay, stuck together
with dried mud.

Of all the days of the week market-day is the most
wonderful. A gathering that occurs at regular intervals
announcing, like an enormous human clock, the lapse of
seven days in which fortunes were made and fortunes were
lost, in which some people earned their wages honestly,
some dishonestly; when some found food in abundance
while others starved. It measures the span of life.

After the fair the vacant lot remains deserted except
for the crows, and stray herds of sheep and goats, and
teams of schoolboys coming in for football.

So, although in the countryside marketplaces are alike
for the most part, it was different in the case of the Saturday market round that area. For that one had a peculiar
characteristic. It had a fence round it made of iron spikes
except for a gap of about two metres where the spikes
were replaced by a sturdy wall made of cement and
rubble.

People had long been speculating about that bit of wall.
They said at first there was a treasure underneath which
led to a cock who would one day crow at the break of
day and bring fortune to whoever found him. But soon the
story faded out. To believe it was like believing in miracles;
a story they repeated from wishful thinking. Then they
said it had been built in order to cover the mouth of a well

from which genii stole to the earth from the underworld.
So the wall was built and a Koran, a *Bokhari*,[1] amulets
and bits of glass were placed inside, which were meant to
hold back the genii. But this story too, like the others,
faded out.

Then came a new generation, less imaginative than the
preceding one, who saw in the wall an abortive attempt to
build the entire fence of cement and rubble.

The people never tired of trying to account for that
incongruous part of the fence. Yet for all that the simple
truth was unbelievable.

That marketplace was never intended to be one in the
first place. It was just a barren piece of land where nothing
would grow. Folk from the neighbouring villages found it
a convenient place where they could meet, laden with
barley and dates and cheese which they exchanged for
calico and bits of mirror and knives fresh from the black-
smith's hand. The land happened to be part of the vast
possessions of an aristocratic landowner from those parts
who was descended from a long line of Turks, or maybe
Mamluks, God only knew.

He was quick to grasp that the presence of those people
and their cattle on his land was profitable; an excellent
means by which to fertilize it and eventually make it fit
for cultivation. So they were permitted to come. In fact
they were encouraged to come when he rode in their midst
on his mare and dispensed his benevolent smiles generously.

When the droppings left behind by the cattle had
accumulated sufficiently to fertilize the land the owner
decided it was time he had it ploughed. But the people
trampled in just the same and left only after they had held
their market and flattened the furrows. He had them
driven away and then ploughed the land again. They were
back the following week, again flattening the furrows.

His old bailiff ventured to point out there was a means
by which he could use the land to better advantage and

---

[1] Well-known collection of the Prophet's sayings.

that was by letting the people carry on their trade as usual
in exchange for a toll. This advice he accepted readily
and the following week his collectors were rampant all over
the grounds collecting the toll. And in order to reduce
expenses and raise the returns, a wooden fence was erected
round the vacant lot with a gate leading out to the agricultural road at which only one collector was stationed.

That's how the Saturday market came to be held.
Business was brisk. They traded in everything conceivable :
from fermented barley-bread and liquorice to livestock.
Soon an extension had to be added in order to accommodate the latter.

One knew it was Saturday when the crowds were seen
crawling down to the vacant lot from all directions. Hundreds of turbans and *gallabiehs* milled about, helter-skelter,
jostling with cowherds, and people on donkeys, or with
baskets on their heads, or simply loitering about.

People from the villages to the west had only to cross
the agricultural road and go through the gate, to be inside
the marketplace. But for those coming from the villages
to the east it was more complicated. For the pathways
sloping down from their villages all converged at the old
water-wheel into a single path ending at a point in the
east fence facing the gate in the west fence. To reach the
door they had to go all the way round the fence, which
they considered to be a needless complication. So a short
cut was improvised by simply knocking down one of the
wooden boards of the fence; all they had to do to get
inside was to slip through the gap. The narrow pathway
was now the principal route to and from the marketplace,
while the gap served as a main entrance.

The owner of the land happened to possess a mansion
overlooking the marketplace much adorned with *mash-
rabiehs*[2] and verandahs and reception rooms and things
of that kind. It seems he was taking the air one day, on
one of his verandahs, when he was horrified to see an

[2] Latticed woodwork.

interminable queue of peasants pouring into the marketplace through the fence. He flew into a rage and ranted
and raved and jumped on his horse and galloped down to
see for himself how this came to happen. When he saw the
gap he ranted and raved again and gave orders that the
broken board be replaced at once.

On the following market-day he stood on his verandah
waiting to gloat over the queue as it broke up when it came
to the blocked entrance. But his fury knew no bounds when
he found them pouring in just the same. Again he dashed
off to the scene and again he found the board had been
removed. They say he had the carpenter who had done
the repair flogged twice : once for having done it badly
and once to make him do it again properly. Furthermore
he stayed and supervised the job himself to see that it was
done to his satisfaction. Only to be appalled the following
week to find that again the board had been removed. He
grew purple with rage and the blood nearly burst out of
his head. This time he ordered two big acacia trees torn
down and chopped up to block the gap.

A week had scarcely gone by before the trees were
flung aside and the queue was pouring in as usual. He
would have burst a vein this time had he not applied a
leech to suck off the blood from his cheeks. And when his
bailiff advised him to spare himself toil and undue irritation
by fixing a proper door to the aperture, he nearly tore
him to pieces. It was no longer a matter of simply fixing
a door but a contest of wills. He wasn't going to be dic-
tated to by a lot of bare-footed vulgar peasants. If before
he had acted on an angry impulse, now he was going to
act according to reason and rational thinking. This took
him all night. By morning he had hit on the idea of hiring
a crew of men from Upper Egypt with their picks and
axes, to dig a deep trench all round the marketplace and
fill it with water. It was done within a week. Being
certain, at last, that he had found the radical solution to
his problem, the man did not bother to stand and watch
the result that week, nor any of the subsequent weeks.

Meanwhile, the chopped-up acacia trees had been hauled back, dumped into the trench, and brought level with the ground by heaping lumps of dried mud on top of them. The very mud that had been dug out in making the trench. Then part of the trench was filled in so that it formed a bridge between the pathway and the old entrance. The owner came upon this during one of his saunters on horseback one day. He could hardly control his rage as he could now see clearly that he was being defied openly by the worthless peasants. He called in three of the tallest and broadest of his guards and threatened to bring ruin upon their heads if it came to his knowledge that a single man had penetrated the fence.

On market-day that week, for the first time the queue was forced to break up. A brawl had started at the entrance after which the broad and the tall were carried back, bleeding, to the mansion. By the end of the day the queue was on the march again down its regular route.

When the guards recovered, they were sent back on duty at the fence. New brawls broke out though less violent than before. The queue slowed down on occasion but soon resumed their march as the guards looked the other way.

One day the landowner came upon his men sitting in the shade of a sycamore tree while gifts came pouring into their laps. So they were sacked and some masons and a load of bricks were brought, and he ordered a wall to be built which would completely seal off the gap. He had hoped, at the same time, to have sealed off any gaps in himself which made him doubt of his success.

One Saturday had barely gone by when the man, distraught with rage, discovered that one of the boards right next to the wall had been wrenched away and a new opening was gaping in its place.

That day he vowed to sell the place. But he had no time to honour his vow, for the Markets Company requisitioned the site by virtue of a decree and long-term instalments. Instead of the old wooden fence the company erected a new one made of iron spikes which were replaced whenever they showed signs of decay. Unlike the previous owner they did not resort to thugs or massive walls but acted in co-operation with the local authorities who appointed a detachment of the cavalry to patrol the grounds every Saturday.

And yet, early on a Saturday morning you will still find the same interminable queue crawling down the pathway and pouring steadily through the fence into the marketplace.

And so, everywhere, there will always be a broken spike.

The Funeral Ceremony

Abou'l Metwalli stood in the doorway of the mosque while the midday sun poured down on him, blistering his white face. It made his hair, snow-white like a rabbit's, glow with the heat, and his bald eyelids, which he tightened against the sunlight, grow redder still. For a while he stood dodging the rays of the sun, unable to see inside except when he craned his neck to push his head into the shade within. He searched the mosque with his bleary eyes until he found the man he was looking for, sitting at the foot of a column fighting off sleep.

'Sheikh Mohamed,' he called in his quiet nasal voice. But his voice was lost in the hum that rose from the prostrated worshippers, ringing in hollow echoes against the lofty walls of the mosque. He raised his voice and struggled to make himself heard, his face reddening with the effort until it was the colour of a cock's comb.

Finally the man heard him and turned his head as if he was expecting to be called. His eyes darted to the door, then he picked himself up and shuffled across. Abou'l Metwalli was relieved as he could now rest his eyes from the strain of searching. He drew his eyelids tightly together again, leaving only a narrow slit from which to follow what was going on.

'What took you so long, Mabrouk?' asked the Sheikh.

Abou'l Metwalli had no time for civilities, he did not trouble to reply. Instead, he placed the bundle he was carrying on the bench that protruded in the doorway. It contained a dead infant wrapped in a faded blanket.

'Read the prayers, Sheikh Mohamed,' he ordered.

The Sheikh demurred. He craned his neck and looked

to the left, then to the right. Then he smiled, an artless
cunning smile, and was starting to say something when
Abou'l Metwalli cut him short irritably.

'Just read the prayers,' he insisted, screwing up his eyes
more tightly, as if in defiance of both Sheikh Mohamed
and the sun. He gave his *gallabieh* a hard smack to mark
his discontent, and tugged at his turban with both hands
to set it straight, perhaps for the hundredth time since the
morning.

He planted himself more firmly in his place until the
Sheikh got started on his prayers. Then he let his attention drift to the petty brawls that were breaking out all
the time between the countless hawkers and their customers
standing all round the mosque. But the sun was in his
eyes so he moved them to the shade where a *zikhr* was in
full sway. The ring included a motley crowd of people
led by a half-witted Sheikh, who wore a red sash and a
leather pouch slung over his shoulder. Only God knew what
was inside. He was leading the *zikhr* by hitting his beads on
an iron tube he was holding, while he kept up a monotonous chant, his voice even more repulsive than his face.

When the liquorice-juice seller came round, and the
clash of his cymbals rang in the air, Abou'l Metwalli suddenly became aware of his parched throat and he couldn't
resist the temptation of the cool beads that glistened on
the glass container. So he held out half a piastre to the
man, and with one breath blew off the foamy top from
the glass he gave him and in the name of Allah gulped
down the liquid. Feeling his soul revive he dug into his
waist pocket again and came up with another half piastre
which he chucked at the man. Once again his throat went
into convulsions as he gulped down the second glass.

It made him belch and his body became drenched in
sweat. He stole a look at the sycamores a man was selling
not far from him, but didn't like the look of them so he
came back to the door to find Sheikh Mohamed nearing
the end of the prayers, having made two prostrations.

'Peace and the mercy of God be with you,' he was saying in peroration as he stared towards the undertaker. His voice was loud and pointed, with a hint of reproof at Abou'l Metwalli. Then he dropped it to a whisper and went on to terminate the prayer. The undertaker eyed him with suspicion.

'Sheikh, would you swear on your Moslem faith that the boy was properly turned towards the *Kiblah*?'[1]

Sheikh Mohamed, ending his prayer, raised his voice. 'God bless and save . . .,' he went on, but the undertaker wouldn't let him.

'Can you say in good faith that your ablutions were correctly performed?'

'. . . and save our lord Mohamed and his Family, and his Companions.' The prayer was ended. 'What is the matter, brother, don't you trust me?' asked the Sheikh. Abou'l Metwalli mumbled something that made no sense even to himself. He picked up the bundle.

'How many does this one make?' the Sheikh was now asking, having wound up the prayer in a hurry.

The undertaker paused, saying nothing for a while as his irritation returned, making his small load feel like a ton of bricks. He had done his best to avoid this issue but now it seemed inevitable.

'This one makes seven, Sheikh Mohamed,' he said slowly.

'What do you mean, seven? I swear by the lady Miska, and Om Hashem and all God's saints, this one makes eight.'

'Seven, I tell you Sheikh Mohamed, and I swear by almighty God.'

'Look here, 'Am[2] Metwalli, you're a man with a family, you can't afford to be dishonest. I swear, I tell you. Alright, let's count them from the beginning. There was that boy you brought from El Hanafi this morning. That makes one. Then there was that girl, your cousin . . .'

'You look here, Sheikh Mohamed, I tell you it's only seven, and if that's not true I'll repudiate my wife.'

[1] Direction of Mecca towards which Moslems turn their faces in prayer.
[2] Uncle. A respectful form of address to an elderly person.

'I tell you, man . . .'

'And I'm telling you, only seven, and if that's not true I'll repudiate my wife.'

'Very well, we'll leave it to your conscience. God is your witness.'

'So how much have you had so far?'

'One ten-piastre piece.'

The undertaker paused to calculate.

'So now for all seven I still owe you four piastres.'

'But . . . I mean, look . . .'

'But what?'

'I mean. . . . Look, do I need to tell you? How much is a pound of tomatoes these days, hey? And okra beans, do you know how much they are? And business so slack. No proper celebrations, no funeral ceremonies, nothing coming in. And the wife, yesterday I had to buy her aspirins . . .'

'Come on, man, don't give me that crap. You ought to be thankful. Summer's coming, and the epidemic won't be far behind, and you're going to be so busy you won't know whether you're coming or going. You've got to trust in God, man. Here, take this.'

Sheikh Mohamed hesitated, clutching and unclutching his hand, before he decided to stretch it out and take the five-piastre note the undertaker was pushing at him. He felt it with his fingers, and shrank his neck deeper inside his robe. He screwed up his eyes and blinked; he rubbed the paper note between his fingers and folded it up and nearly gave it back but thought better of it. He peered through the mist that veiled his eyes.

'Alright, Mabrouk, I'll have one piastre more.'

But nobody heard him because Abou'l Metwalli and his bundle had already vanished in the crowd.

All on a Summer's Night

Evening prayers were over. The hay was cold and piled high, and the night was dark and silvery. There was a grave and the clouds drifted over it fluttering in the air like the soft white handkerchiefs of lovers. Nearby lay our town crouching like a hedgehog, with its thorns, and sorrows, and trees, and we were there on the hay, talking, not like the grown-ups ruminating on their troubles, but mostly about ourselves. A dark force was just beginning to devastate our bodies, working a change in us which grew daily more evident and which we sensed with mixed feelings of joy and bewilderment.

Although we had many troubles we never talked about them. We worked as hard as the men, perhaps harder, for they were inclined to be indolent, sitting in the shade while they left us to broil toiling in the fields. Sometimes they begged us, sometimes they ordered us but in either case we were happy. To work was to be a man, and that's what we longed to be, and if we were made to work it meant we had grown up and that we were dependable and in the prime of life, with promise in our future. Soon we would marry and there would be processions and wedding feasts and celebrations in our honour.

Having toiled all day we had voracious appetites. We devoured anything in sight and our mothers thrilled to see we were growing, and they'd feed us on the sly, much as they forcibly fed their ducks and their geese, keeping for us the choicest meats and eggs and cheese. We were growing fast, as though to make up for lost time, shaking off the paleness of a long childhood and the lean years. Our faces filled out taking the colour of rich silt, our legs grew tougher, and our throats became thicker as our voices broke.

We used to sit together on the hay in the evenings, our bodies a prey to that force which made us listless, neither giving ourselves up to dreams nor yet able to curb its powerful drive. The night shuddered with our voices and our new virility as we sat in that distant spot giving vent to thoughts we dared not voice except there where we smothered ourselves in the comforting coolness of the hay.

Conversation came of itself. No one knew how it started but when it did it flowed on without end. The night was a refuge. We loved it like a beautiful woman who stirred our sleeping passions, soft and tender and ebony black, much as we hated the harsh and forbidding light of day.

We used to measure ourselves the moment we got together, each one trying to prove he was the tallest. We made bets and the loser pretended he had a pain and a swelling in the thigh which he showed the others who assured him there was no reason to worry; the swelling only meant he was growing. And then we'd go on to describe the dreams that we dreamt, or to compare our voices, feeling one another's throats. But invariably we ended up talking about women. The women of our town were like the majority of its dwellings, dark and flat and without curves. Some houses, though, were whitewashed, and we loved to imagine there was a beautiful woman inside every white house. It was about them, mostly, that we talked. For beautiful women must be easy to get, we decided, or else there was no point in their being beautiful.

Sometimes we ran wild with our imagination, working ourselves up to a mad pitch of excitement and we would start throwing hay at one another and roll about and shout and howl like wolves. But soon we were forced to calm down before we were discovered by some watchman who would send us home where there was nothing but to flop on our pallets on top of the oven and fight off the lonesomeness and the bafflement and the demons inside us that prevented sleep. Only there on the haystack, with one another, were the demons becalmed, and we found relief talking to one another.

Mohamed was the pivot on whom we all hinged. He was older but no less bewildered than the rest of us although he was more experienced. He had left our town at an early age to go to work in the city. He was always in the thick of things and he always had something to tell. What's more he knew about women, which was more than any of us could boast. None of us had any real experience of women. At most we ogled them from a distance, fearing and desiring them at the same time but quailing at the thought of anything more intimate. So we loved to listen to Mohamed, and we avidly lapped up the tales he used to tell us about his exploits. We were quite fond of him with his sprouting moustache and his long hair which he was allowed to grow as he pleased while we were forced by our fathers to crop ours short. He had a blond forelock which he was fond of smearing with vaseline borrowed from the station-master, or failing that, with butter. His woollen skull-cap was always tilted back on his head to show off his shining forelock. He also had a hare-lip that made him appear truculent, which in reality he wasn't. He was jolly and good-natured and full of fun, and his skin was untanned by the scorching sun of the fields. He used to till the land at one time until he went to the city for some reason, and having had a taste of it vowed never to return to the plough. Sometimes as we sat with him we couldn't help feeling he was not one of us but some stranger. One of those fast and clear-witted boys from the city whom we dreaded so much. On the whole we were not given to wrong-doing and we feared transgression, but we were emboldened by his example. It was he who showed us how to fill our laps with rubble as we entered our homes and replace it with corn or barley or cotton, and walk out unsuspected. It was he who arranged to sell the loot, keeping a portion of the gains for himself and with what was left we would buy ourselves *halva* and tangerines and bamboo canes with which we loved to swagger on market-days.

That night we were sitting together, just a handful of boys from the town, their muddy feet full of cracks, their clothes in rags, their faces an indefinite blur of tanned hide. We sat exhaling odours of our dinner in the light summer air : onions and cheese and pickled peppers and sardines and leeks. The wheat was all around us, some of it swaying in the fields, some of it already tied in sheaves and lined up in small bundles like rows of prostrated worshippers. Nearby the threshing machine crouched like a kneeling camel, and the scent of the new crop floated in the air mingling with the smell of the earth, wet with dew, and the reek of our sweat which, like ourselves, had suffered a change, acquiring an odour which was intensely male.

It was nights such as this that gave Mohamed's talk its peculiar fascination. His voice, where a manly ring had already settled, unlike ours, was steady, and he held us spellbound by his manner of recounting a story. He told us about many places, near and far, some of which we knew, some we didn't, nor he himself for that matter. Strange, exotic places which called up visions of well-dressed people, and railways, and tall buildings. We usually kept him till the end, after we had exhausted our own stock of gossip about our town, and its women, and how we ogled them, and how they ogled us. And then we would let Mohamed take over.

That night we could tell from the way he began that he wanted to tell us about the bedouin woman he had met at the village fair. But we stopped him when we saw he was beginning to cheat, rehashing things we had heard before. We wanted something new for we knew him by now. He had a trick of starting with a lengthy preamble then stopping abruptly in the middle so that we would coax him to go on, promising wheat and maize and eggs in return. Sometimes too he would clam up suddenly for no reason and nothing we said would make him change his mind.

'Listen boys,' he began that night. 'I'm going to tell you something that happened to me on condition you don't breathe a word of it to anyone.'

'Promise.'

'You swear on God's Holy Book?'

'Swear.'

'And anyone who squeals . . .'

'Is a stinking creep.'

'And the son of a dog.'

'The son of a dog.'

'Well,' he began. 'I was going to Mansourah one day, on business . . .'

'Liar, you've never been to Mansourah.'

'I have, I swear on the Holy Book.'

We believed him, panting with excitement. We couldn't help it. He was going to tell us about Mansourah which none of us had ever seen. But we had all heard about it, all sorts of fantastic things. We imagined it to be a vast Garden of Eden, full of Europeans and milk-white girls, and women draped in shiny *melayas*[1] that shimmered when they walked. We imagined their bodies to be boneless, and their flesh soft and malleable like Turkish delight. We imagined their men to be sops; no match for their women who desired real men. Men like ourselves, coarse peasants with the strength of a bull.

'Go on,' we said to Mohamed.

After he got off the train, he said, he had seen to the business that took him there, and seeing he still had some time left before he caught the train back, he bought himself a loaf of bread to eat while he took a stroll down the road where the station was. It was full of big houses with large verandahs. It was late afternoon and most of the women were out taking the air. Bunches of them; had they been dealt out to the men in our town each man would have come out with a cluster.

Well, as he was going along, his eye was caught by one verandah where a women was leaning over the railing wearing a red dressing gown.

'What's a dressing gown?'

---

[1] Black silk covering worn by many women.

'Oh, something like a robe.'

We were always sceptical of the things he said. We listened to him like magistrates oscillating between belief and disbelief. There was always a suspicion he was pulling our legs.

Mohamed went on with his story. He was just passing under that balcony, he said, when the woman smiled at him. He thought she was smiling at someone else but the street was deserted except for himself and when he looked back at her she smiled again. We grabbed Mohamed by his *gallabieh*.

'Careful now, don't you leave anything out,' we said, gasping.

'Don't worry. I'll tell you everything.'

It didn't matter whether his story were true or not as long as he kept on with it.

'Well,' he continued, 'she smiled again, boys, and my heart began to pound, and I said to myself, this is your lucky day, boy. I pretended I didn't notice and looked at her again and she laughed. I could do with a glass of *zibib*, I thought to myself.'

'What's *zibib*?'

'That's brandy, boys.'

'And what's brandy?'

'That's drink, liquor.'

Here, we got afraid. Mohamed taking liquor? We allowed him women, but not liquor. However, for Mohamed's sake we were willing to close an eye to that.

'Then what.'

'I found a tavern open, owned by a European. So I went in. 'Hey, mister,' I said. 'Yes,' he said. 'Give me a *zibib*. I want the real stuff. And I want cucumbers for a snack.'

'Snack? What's that?'

'Cucumbers.'

We didn't dare repeat the question, as we were more anxious to hear what was coming.

'I drank it up, and what do you think? It turned me on.

My blood caught fire. And to make double sure I ordered another one before I took myself back to her street.'

'And you went past her house again?'

'I did.'

'And she smiled at you?'

'A smile that gave wings to my soul, boys. One hell of a beautiful woman, and she was wearing . . .'

'What?'

'She was wearing embroidered clogs, and I could see the curves of her body under her dressing gown, and she was smiling. So I looked at her and smiled. So she smiled back.'

'What for?'

'Well, I was in my best clothes. My camel-hair cap, and patent leather shoes, and my silk scarf was draped over my shoulder. Besides, I'm quite a smasher, don't forget, being young and all that. Well, I gave her a wink so she went inside and came back wearing a new dressing gown, of green silk. Then she signalled to me to come upstairs.'

'Upstairs?'

'That's right. I must say, though, I was a little shaky. I was a stranger, after all, entering a strange house just to see a woman. Suppose I were caught, where would I be? Or suppose she had relatives. Anyway, I went up. It was the two *zibibs* that did it.'

'And you went inside her house?'

'Can't you be patient? I rang the bell . . .'

'What bell?'

'A bell at the door, with a push button . . .'

'A bell with a push button?'

'You ignorant peasant clots. You'll never learn. Of course, stupid, bells have buttons. Well, she opened the door and told me to come in . . . a voice like spun sugar . . .'

'And you went in?'

'Stop interrupting or I won't tell.'

'Alright, go on.'

'I stood at the door, a little uncertain. 'Come on,' she

said, 'don't be afraid, my husband is away.' So I said to
myself, "Come on, boy, get yourself in, you only die once".'
    'That's right, Mohamed, damn you. Go right in.'
    'So I went in, and sat in the sitting-room. Gilt chairs,
boys, fit for a king, and mirrors on the walls, and coloured
baubles and things. After a while I found her coming in
wearing a navy blue dress, something out of this world.
She had a bottle and two glasses with her. She said, "What's
your name, young man?" 'Your servant, Mohamed,' I
replied. "You're my master," she said. "Bless you. Would
you like to sit on the chair, or just make yourself comfort-
able, wherever you like . . ." '
    'The chair, of course, you fool.'
    'No. I'm not used to sitting on chairs. I was afraid it
might make me dizzy. Well, then I asked what her name
was. "Fifi," she said, and then she asked if I would have a
drink, and I said yes and we sat drinking, glass after glass
until the room began to spin. "What's the matter?" she
asked. "Are you getting tight?" "Oh, no," I replied.
"Would you like something to sober you up?" she asked.
I didn't dare say yes.'
    'Silly boy. And did she get you anything?'
    'You bet. I found her coming in with a huge tray loaded
with food.'
    'What was on it?'
    'Turkey stuffed with pigeon, and roast potatoes, and
mutton.'
    'You lucky devil! And you ate all that?'
    'I didn't know what I was doing. She just kept feeding
me . . .'
    'Have you no shame, boy?'
    'Shame, my foot. I was all wound up and I stretched
my hand and I touched her.'
    'Without washing your hands?'
    'I washed them, damn you. Look, who's telling this
story? I'm getting tired of you.'
    We begged him to go on, although he didn't need to be
begged. He was so carried away with his tale nothing

could have stopped him.

'I touched her, boys, and her flesh was like honey paste.'

'Was her skin fair?'

'Fairer than beaten cotton.'

'And her hair, was it black?'

'Black as pitch, down to her knees.'

'Go on, tell, boy, what else? Mind you don't skip anything.'

'And her skin, boys! It was smooth and soft as silk. I said, "Please, I can't stand it any longer." She said, "Alright, come along." And she took me to the bed, and let down the mosquito-net. It was pink, I swear, and then she turned off the light.'

'Easy now, mind you go slowly.'

'Well, and I looked and saw the mosquito-net was shimmering. It must be doomsday, I thought to myself. And you know what? She had turned on another light inside the mosquito-net. There were small coloured bulbs at the top, red, green, blue, yellow . . . and I looked and saw her before me, gorgeous, bewitching. She was all coloured, like a sprite . . .'

'Then what?'

'Then nothing. Boy, what a night! Better than anything in *The Arabian Nights*.'

'What happened? Go on, you've got to tell. What happened next?'

'Nothing. That's all.'

'Come on, what happened next? Don't be mean, boy.'

He condescended to add a thing or two which did nothing to satisfy our curiosity.

'Leave him alone, he's fibbing,' said one boy.

'Swear all this is true,' said another.

Mohamed swore and we got even more excited. We did not believe him. He swore on his mother's grave that what he told us was true, every bit of it.

'Did I ever lie to you?' he asked.

'You're lying now.'

'Alright, have it your way.'

'Suppose we go to Mansourah, will you take us to the place?'

'Sure.'

'Alright, let's go now. Right away.'

That was a great idea. We raised a roar and cheered and yelled and shouted as we pushed and shoved one another. We got hold of Mohamed by his arms and legs and swung him about then tossed him up on the haystack. Then we took a spin on the threshing machine. We had gone quite wild. Little clouds of hay blew up in the air and settled in our eyes and covered us with dust.

'Come on boys, off to Mansourah.'

'Off to Mansourah!' everybody shouted.

'It's too dark boys.'

'And all the digging to be done tomorrow . . .'

But nothing was going to keep us from going to Mansourah, and we started off.

After having walked for a while we realized we had covered a large part of the way. Our town lay behind with its borders and its fields. Only then did we realize we were actually on our way to Mansourah. Already we could smell foreign soil beneath our feet. It felt different back home where everything was familiar and we moved freely. Every palm tree, every field, every house where we had played and romped in our childhood was familiar, and every man was our kin. Each one of us, blindfold, could tell the soil of our town from that of another. Suddenly we knew we were far from home.

We were seized with panic as we stared into the dark and realized we did not know where the road was leading us. But none of us dared voice his fear. We moved on in a mass like an enormous giant with multiple heads and arms and legs, trying to melt our fears in the shelter of one another. We continued on our impetuous march, glum, silent, unbridled by reason, drawn by the magic call of Mansourah, driven in spite of ourselves.

There was only the dull sound of our bare feet on the road, like a caravan of camels. Those of us wearing shoes

had long removed them and carried them tucked under
their arms. We were gasping, our faces were shining and
dust kept blowing up in our wake. The night was huge
and black and fearful, full of secret whispers. The planta-
tions stretched like a vast shoreless sea. The crops stood
still, moving only with the breeze, slowly, inanimately.
Water-wheels creaked from afar like mourners bewailing a
corpse. Gunshots sounded in the distance, out of nowhere
into nowhere, and cocks crowed before their time. The
barking of dogs came from reaches unknown, and a vast
wind blew over a vast land, and the earth murmured, and
obscure whispers came up from obscure places, sly and
treacherous like the sound of huge whales twisting and
turning in a sea of darkness.

Someone stretched a hand and jabbed another in the
ribs and he jumped with a yell. Soon it caught on, and
we were all in an uproar, shouting, jumping, and falling
all over one another.

'What about her legs, Mohamed? Did she have legs
like ours?'

'You call those tree stumps legs, man?'

'What were hers like?'

'Milk white.'

'Like Safeya's, the dancing girl?'

'Don't be an ass, Safeya's not a patch on her.'

'And did she have a fish tattooed on her belly?'

'What fish, you fool! What are you talking about?'

'Well what did she have on her belly?'

'Nothing. A belly like hers is not made for a tattoo.'

'And was her face painted?'

'I didn't notice.'

'How come, silly? Didn't you look?'

'I think it was.'

'And what's her talk like? Does she speak like city folk,
or like us?'

'Like city folk, of course.'

We all broke into a riot again. The woman had taken
substance and she was standing alive before our minds'

eye, beautiful, palpable, just as we desired her.

We jogged on, pushing and shoving and laughing and talking. Every now and then we'd make a guess as to how long it would be before we reached Mansourah.

Suddenly we realized Mohamed had disappeared.

The shock was like a stab. We shot out wildly in all directions to catch him. Any doubt that he was telling the truth vanished. Every little detail of his story was indelibly engraved upon our minds. The lady of the red gown and the bottle became a vivid reality not just another creation of Mohamed's brain. She was the woman each one of us already possessed. She was going to swoon with happiness when one after the other we were going to climb up to her iron-railed balcony. In her joy she was even going to give us each a one-pound note, for we were the strapping braves unmatched in all Mansourah.

And the swine goes and disappears!

We spread ourselves out in a tight network. By the graveyard, and the railway line, and the bridge. We were not going to let this whole venture come to nothing when Mansourah was already within reach. Another stretch and we would find our quest. Hundreds of European women, milk-white, and so beautiful you could eat them alive, sweeter to the taste than bees' honey and cream.

'There he is boys,' came a shout from the distance.

We flew in the direction of the voice and there we found Mohamed struggling with the boy who'd caught him. We threw ourselves on top of him. It wasn't difficult to pin him down. He fought vigorously, dealing out powerful blows like a man's. But we closed in on him like an army of ants attacking a breadcrumb, until at last he was overpowered and he ceased to struggle. One boy ripped off his *gallabieh* and tied him with it.

'What do you want now?' asked Mohamed defiantly.

'You're going to show us that place.'

'I won't.'

'Yes you will.'

'You can't force me.'

'You wait and see.'

'I'll show you, you effeminate lot of bastards!'

'Get up!'

He held fast to the ground and we dragged him up by force while he spluttered out angrily: 'It's a long way to Mansourah, I tell you.'

'That's none of your business.'

'I'm warning you. Don't say I didn't tell you.'

We walked on in silence, all of us tense and on edge. We thought of singing to relieve the tension. But we didn't know any songs. Only the girls were any good at singing. One boy knew the first line of an old lay and he started to sing it but his voice was so ugly we made him shut up. Tiny luminous dots were beginning to speckle the horizon like the eyes of grasshoppers when they catch the light. They were the lights of Mansourah which meant we were almost there. We broke into a run dragging Mohamed along until we were out of breath. Then we slowed to a walking pace. We walked a long time and still the lights were no closer, almost as if the nearer we approached the farther they receded, sinking in the dark.

'Let's go back boys,' said Mohamed.

'Shut up, you. Hurry up boys, it's getting late.'

We summoned the remainder of our strength and walked on. All of a sudden a great peal of laughter cut through the emptiness of the road. It was Mohamed. He was doubled up, unable to control himself, and when he saw us looking at him he forced himself into new convulsions.

'I got you!' he was saying between gasps. 'You bunch of idiots, I got you!'

'What do you mean?'

'You blinking bunch of idiots. You believed everything I said. I never went near Mansourah, and I never saw any woman.'

'Liar!'

'I swear boys, I never even saw Mansourah.'

'You son of a dog!'

'And you blinking idiots!'

A heavy silence fell upon us as we stared at the lights of Mansourah which now seemed to be within reach of our hands. To our fevered imagination the town became the embodiment of a woman with flesh like soft dough, draped in a dressing gown and leaning out from a balcony, beckoning for us to come. We looked back at Mohamed and found him still laughing in scorn.

'He's pulling your leg,' someone said.

'He won't show us the woman. He doesn't want us to see the place.'

'What do you mean, you swine?' snapped Mohamed angrily.

We swore at him saying we weren't going to let him go until he took us to the house. He swore back, and scoffed, and called us fools and idiots. We vowed we weren't going to let him get away with it, he wasn't going to keep the woman to himself. We ordered him to walk on, but he refused so we dragged him. He kicked one of the boys in the stomach and started lashing out wildly with his hands and his legs. We fell on him in a mass and forced him to the ground, punching at him, slapping his face. He resisted, hitting back savagely until he was overcome and we tied him down again. We smeared his face with mud and somebody spat on him. He tried to shout but we gagged him. For a moment it looked as if he was going to choke to death so we relaxed our grip a little to let him breathe.

'Drag him to the field and brand him with fire, boys,' someone suggested.

'Yes, let's.' And we dragged him into a field and started to look for matches but we found none. We'll make a spark, we decided, and started to look for flint and found some over the railway line. Now we needed a nail or a piece of iron. We found only a scrap of tin. One boy crouched on Mohamad's chest and ran the piece of tin across his legs.

'Are you going to show us that woman's house, or do you want to die?' He made no reply. We dug our nails into his flesh and scratched. Then we bit him. But he still wouldn't tell. We realized at last it was no use, that he had been lying all along and we renewed the attack with savage fury.

'Come on, say it, say you're a sissy,' hissed the boy who held the tin.

Mohamed only kicked at him and cursed our fathers in return.

'Alright, give it to him, boys.' And we got to work on the flint trying to produce a spark. A tiny part of ourselves couldn't help admiring his guts, but for the most part we hated him for having fooled us all that time.

At last we obtained a spark and it caught on the piece of cotton. We cheered and blew on it. It was a pale, wan, cold fire. We blew harder but it only grew paler. No matter how hard we blew, the fire remained wan and cold.

Not only the fire but everything all around was starting to wane. Then something whistled in our ears like a cry for help, and we realized with horror that we were in the midst of something dreadful. We stared at one another in a daze as slowly we began to wake to the stark reality. Our faces were bruised and grubby, and our clothes were covered with dust. And flies. Thousands of sticky flies droned and flew around us incessantly.

How did we come to this torment? What were our people going to say? Surely we would be beaten and roundly abused when we returned. Some of us would have to rise at dawn; there were the water-wheels to be assembled, and the barns to be cleaned, and we'd had no sleep, and our eyes were bloodshot. Had they caught some infection? Was the sun also rising on our town, back home? Why was there shock on our faces, and guilt, and remorse? Why were they blotched and diseased and ravaged with pimples? Why did we realize only now that we were wretchedly poor, and that there was nothing in our homes but barking dogs and roaring fathers and screeching mothers and the suffocating smoke of the stove?

Horrified, we began to feel our bodies and examine our clothes to see how much damage was done. We saw our-

selves with appalling clarity which made us fear to look
at the core inside.

Mohamed lay on the road like a slaughtered beast, his
gallabieh in shreds, his body limp and covered with flies.
Gory wounds gaped from his flesh and the blood clotted
on his nose and down the side of his mouth and inside the
cleft of his hare-lip. Slowly, dispassionately, we loosed his
bonds. He groaned with pain and our hearts went out to
him.

Once more we found ourselves roaming, back on the
same road that saw us coming, driven in spite of ourselves.
We were limping and groaning and leaning on one another.
Our thoughts were dwelling on the coming dawn, rising
suddenly, giving shape to the earth, with grief and care
in its folds. And the harsh inexorable day loomed ahead
like a huge monster, bigger than the sun. Stark and merciless, awaiting, threatening, his eyes spitting fire as we
approached, awed and quivering, knowing full well there
was no escape.

The Caller in the Night

It was Hagg Sa'ad's funeral ceremony. The time was just after the evening prayers when most people begin to arrive. A modest tent had been erected to receive the guests. It was lit by gas lamps that gave a pale, anaemic light. They shone brightly just the same, through the blackness that enveloped our village, guiding the crowds of fellahin who came to bring their condolences. They were not used to lights by night so that they were momentarily blinded the moment they stepped inside and it was some time before they could recognize any of the people sitting there. The front seats, made of tarnished gilt with chipped edges and covered by worn faded velvet, were occupied as usual by the prominent personalities of the town.

I was considered the most highly educated man there because I was a student of medicine. Everyone insisted on calling me Doctor. The people adopted me, so to speak, and looked upon me as something of a local treasure of which they boasted to the other towns. When they went to market, the women would say arrogantly to those from elsewhere, 'Shut up, woman, at least we have doctors in our town.' And children at play stopped to stare when they saw me coming. 'He's a doctor, boys, a real one,' they'd say to one another. Adults followed me with their eyes and called blessings on me, and asked God to guard me from the evil eye and make me a joy to my father.

So, being elevated to the ranks of the prominent, it was my right and my duty to sit with them although like most others who were educated I would have preferred to sit with the majority who were poor fellahin. Hagg Sa'ad, God

63

rest his soul, used to say of them that they were made of
the rubble left over after God created the brainy folks
from the soft clay of paradise.

We would rather have sat with them, as I said, because
there we could be more relaxed, and we did not need to
put a strain on our speech or behaviour as anything we said
was sure to go down as holy writ.

I was sitting in the corner near the entrance with some
university students and a large number of date-palm clippers when a new group of people, who made it a point
always to be seen with the educated, came and joined us.
They were headed by Abou Ebeid, the orderly from the
fever hospital who liked to have what he called 'the
medical corps' sitting together in one place. He too prac-
tised medicine, in a way. He examined patients, and made
diagnoses, and give injections. He wore a clean white over-
all, a cotton *gallabieh* and a tarboosh, and I must say he
looked smarter in that outfit than any of the rest of us.

The last one to join us was Abdallah the barber who
passed as a doctor too since besides shaving people and
giving them haircuts he performed such things as circum-
cisions and bleedings and treated boils as well. When he
saw us sitting anywhere he would give his shaving kit
quickly to his assistant and order him to sit with it somewhere out of sight as though he wanted to shed his identity
as a barber. Then he would come and join us with profuse
greetings, most notably to me. 'You have honoured us,
Doctor,' he would say. He was careful to pronounce the
word 'doctor' correctly with two short o's to prove to me
and the others that he was enlightened and that for this
reason he had a right to claim affinity to the medical profession.

We were sitting in silence, having resigned ourselves to
the ugly voice of Sheikh Moustapha, the village Koran
chanter, as it poured on us in flat tones that came through
his nose. It didn't look as if he intended to stop soon. Every
time he reached a cadence we thought that was the end,
only to be flooded with fresh notes while he craned his

neck, and frowned, and placed his hand over his right ear
and strained until we thought the veins in his neck would
burst. Then he would let out such a loud wail that it
pierced right through the darkness, waking the sleepers
in the next village and making ours shake. The only person
allowed to move freely during a funeral ceremony was the
head watchman. With his rifle slung on his shoulder he
sauntered about in the tent to show people that the law
was present. Then he would dash outside to pounce on the
children who had collected to watch the ceremony and look
at the petrol lamps and the fascinating patterns on the tent,
and he would hack at them with his stick.

Finally we were delivered of Sheikh Moustapha's voice
and his chanting came to an end. The people rushed up to
thank him for his reading with voluble invocations for God
to guard him and protect him from evil.

Soon after, the tent began to hum with the sound of
voices as the various groups resumed their conversation in
low whispers. We began to chat too, beginning with Sheikh
Moustapha and what we thought of him, then we went
on to gossip about the important people of the town and
ended with recollections from Cairo. The fellahin could
only look on and listen, keeping well out of the conversation. They followed our discussions, fascinated by the way
we pronounced our words, while with their eyes they felt
the quality of our zephyr *gallabiehs*, and closely examined
Abou Ebeid's tarboosh and my wrist-watch as it flashed
about reflecting the light. The infinite admiration they had
for us and their absolute faith in everything we said was
clearly reflected on their faces. As for Abou Ebeid, every
time we happened to meet he never missed the chance to
ask me some question, invariably related to medicine. Since
he gave treatment to the fellahin himself, he was anxious
to show them he was a great man of learning who argued
with the Doctor as an equal. He was always careful to
drop his local dialect and affect the genteel accent of the
townspeople, so as not to put himself on a level with
peasants. His tone was bland and unctuous; the same tone

he used when he imposed his services on people, asking
for a little milk in return or a plate of okra beans in addition to his fee. Clients' okra beans were always very good.

He irritated me. I was doing my preparatory year for
medicine that year. Most of my work consisted of dissecting
frogs and studying worms, and I knew nothing yet about
drugs or disease. From his long experience working in
hospitals Abou Ebeid had picked up the technical terms
for a couple of diseases as well as the names of many drugs.
He was discussing Hagg Sa'ad's long illness that night and
how Dr Hanna, the doctor from the central town, had
failed to cure him and how he, Abou Ebeid, had prescribed
'Seteromycin' injections and 'Sulphata Yazin'[1] 3x3x5 (that's
how he put it) as well as M. Alkaline, and ordered him to
abstain from food altogether. But the poor fellow was
seized with a sudden longing for salted fish, of which he
ate a whole pound all by himself, whereupon he expired.
This drew a lot of comment, for the subject of fate and
destiny was one which the fellahin were equal to discussing
and which they loved to ponder on.

'You don't live a day longer than it is written. . . .'

'God in His wisdom. . . .' And so on.

When Abou Ebeid got started on a subject nothing would
make him stop, and he went on to tell us what happened
after the man died. It was he, he told us, who got the burial
licence in spite of the obstacles the doctor was raising; he
even got it after hours, he said, and if it hadn't been for
his clever handling of the situation the man would have
remained without burial till the following day. I don't
remember how we got to leave him out of the conversation
and confine it to ourselves alone. But I remember a discussion about the body and how long it could remain without burial. When the arguments died down, Abou Ebeid
turned to me with a very serious expression on his face.

'Tell me, Doctor,' he began. He too was careful to
pronounce 'doctor' correctly in order to distinguish himself

[1] Attempts at pronouncing the names of the original drugs.

from the fellahin who could never learn not to say 'dactoor'.

I turned to him, prepared to hear some silly question. 'How long after death does rigor mortis set in?' he asked me.

Everybody was terribly impressed by that expression, 'rigor mortis'. Even the barber was astounded at Abou Ebeid's learning. He looked at him with surprise and envy as though he begrudged him that much erudition. All eyes were on me now, waiting for the answer. I was most embarrassed for I hadn't the faintest idea what the expression could mean. I gave a faint smile.

'Why do you ask?' I said, stalling.

'Well, you see,' he said with the air of someone throwing up a public issue for discussion, 'I had a little argument today with Dr Sobhi. You know, the chief medical officer. I was of the opinion that it set in within half an hour, while he insisted it was two hours. What do you say, Doctor?'

I took on a knowing air.

'You're both wrong,' I said, 'actually it sets in after about one hour.'

I looked at the others and saw they were lapping up what I was saying, even though they had no idea what it was all about. There was a brief silence, and I looked at Abou Ebeid to see whether he was satisfied with the answer I gave. His eyes were on the ground, very politely avoiding mine.

I knew that confounded expression of his which he put on every time he found me in a corner, so as not to embarrass me, as it didn't do for a doctor to be embarrassed by a mere orderly.

'I say, Doctor, what's this . . . this "moris rigo?"' asked Saleh suddenly, screwing up his eyes.

Saleh was a fellah, but he was only a hireling. I believe he belonged to the family of Abou Shendi. He worked in return for food and clothing, and perhaps a small share of the annual crop. His skin was the colour of dust and he was so fearfully huge that people called him the Sphinx.

I don't remember ever seeing him smile, or with his eyes fully open. It was almost as if he looked with his eyelashes. They say his heart was dead because he never felt joy or sorrow or fear, and that he was the strongest man in town although he seldom displayed his strength, a little from modesty, and a little from fear of God. He spoke slowly as though every word were wrenched from him and he enjoyed the company of the educated even though he never joined their conversation. People knew he was a silent man on the whole and no one ever provoked him for fear of his mighty blows. He was never known to lose his temper, or grumble, or complain about anything.

Had not the occasion been a sad one we might well have laughed at this sudden question. As it was, the Sphinx was only asking what everyone else wanted to know, and they all turned to me to hear what I was going to say. All except Abou Ebeid who was telling me with his grin that he could answer that one. I scowled, warning him to shut up.

'Well, you see, Saleh,' I said, offhand, 'the human body is a strange thing,' and I rambled on about how the blood circulated in the body, and what made the heart beat and I went on to describe several other functions. I paused to see how this was going down and whether they had forgotten the question. But Saleh screwed up his eyes again.

'But what's this "moris" the Effendi is talking about?' he insisted.

Abou Ebeid was still flashing his cold smile at me. 'That'll teach you,' he seemed to be saying. When he saw I did not answer Saleh immediately he volunteered.

'With your permission, Doctor. Well, you see, folks, a human being is all filled inside with lime and iron and arsenic and mercuric chloride, and Markuro Cron . . . and as long as we are alive these things float about in our bodies, but as soon as a person dies they sort of get stuck together in a lump, as you might say, like a mud pie, so that when you come to feel a dead body with your hands you will find it feels exactly like a plank of wood.'

What he was saying was so preposterous they would not allow themselves to believe it until I approved. They turned to me and waited. I could think of nothing by which to refute Abou Ebeid's learning, so I nodded, which they took for acquiescence. Only then did their remarks come, all in the same breath.

'After all, a man's nothing but carrion.'

'By God, who'd have thought it?'

'Why don't you go and die, Saleh boy, so we can strew the barn with your remains, hey?'

'Just be thankful for your daily bread, and the air you breathe, you bastards.'

Abou Ebeid by now had certainly stolen the show. Everyone was looking at him with awe, as if he had the power to strike them all with rigor mortis. That was more than I could take, and soon I found myself declaiming on the subject of death and corpses with the air of an expert. I found myself telling them tales about what went on in the Faculty morgue and how we slashed at the bodies with our scalpels and how we gutted out bellies, although I had never been near a morgue in my life. They were all so entranced by my fabrications that they forgot all about Abou Ebeid and the funeral ceremony.

Meanwhile a huge man had seated himself on the reader's bench. He was wearing a caftan and cloak. I recognized him to be Sheikh Abdel Hamid, the local preacher. It must be admitted the man was very devoted to his work. He had made himself very popular, never failing to attend every funeral ceremony in the village. He never failed to occupy the reader's bench either, the moment he had a chance, walking up to it with a staid and dignified air.

'In the name of God, the Merciful, the Compassionate,' he began. A deep hush fell on the people as they craned their necks to catch every word. They followed his sermon with great attention. He spoke in deep tones, every syllable loud and clear. Listening to his ringing voice and looking at his ruddy face anyone could see he was a well-fed man,

and a glutton. There was no trace of care in his voice or
evidence that he was burdened by wife or child. Surely a
man destined for paradise in the world to come.

I was supposed to keep silent and listen to the sermon
like everyone else but then I had embarked on a subject
in which Abou Ebeid did not stand a chance against me,
and I was keen to make an impression.

He was familiar with drugs and injections and high-
sounding technical terms, but when it came to corpses only
a doctor was competent. And so I went on with my
discourse while the people divided themselves. The majority
followed the sermon while the rest preferred to listen to
me. I was speaking with an ear cocked to the sermon.
The preacher was declaiming about the punishment awaiting the iniquitous in the hereafter and everyone seemed to
be in a trance. I mean it was the palm-tree clippers who
were more particularly impressed. The higher-ranking
were starting to yawn, and to look at their watches, and
were arguing about the right time. The preacher's haggard
and desiccated audience sat nailed to their seats, their pale
faces wilted like cotton leaves devastated by plant pests,
their mouths gaping, their eyes bloodshot from trachoma.
They were dodging the glare of the petrol lamps the better
to concentrate on the preacher's lurid descriptions of the
tortures reserved for sinners. How they were going to be
delivered to four colossal demons who were going to
make them strip and lash them with a scourge made of
iron with prongs that dug into their flesh and crushed
their bones. Then they were going to be moved to an
upper storey where they would be thrown into a blazing
furnace. Every time the skin burned off, a new layer would
form to prolong the torture, and when they thirsted they
were going to be given the water of hell to drink, which
was made of burning lava.

They followed raptly, hardly knowing what a scourge
was, or lava, or a furnace. Nevertheless the Sheikh's
powerful rhetoric and the strange and terrifying things he
recounted had moved them to tears.

Meanwhile my imagination was running away with me beyond the bounds of credibility. I told my listeners how we thought nothing of taking our meals next to a gutted belly, and how we played cards on top of a dead man's chest, and that I was fond of carving inkwells and rulers and pencils out of skulls and human bones. I told them a tall story about an arm I had once bought from the morgue janitor and how it had caused a scare when I took it home with me to my room.

'And how much did you pay for it, Doctor?' asked the Sphinx, unable to contain himself any longer.

I pretended I was trying to remember.

'Something like twenty piastres, I think,' I said.

'Well! For heaven's sake! Then how much is a whole body?' he asked in amazement.

'I've never bought one,' I said, shrugging, 'but I should think something near a pound or two.'

'And where do they get these bodies?' asked the Sphinx, getting suddenly animated.

I hadn't the slightest idea, but I made out there was a contractor for them just like the one who supplied us with frogs during our preparatory year.

Meanwhile Sheikh Abdel Hamid had reached the end of his sermon. The people had by now utterly lost patience, having listened for hours to the Sheikh's gruesome descriptions. When in peroration he exempted 'those who fear their God' from the horrors he described, a great roar went up as the people sighed with relief at this hope of acquittal.

I saw Sheikh Abdel Hamid turn his plump face, clustered with sweat, to look at his audience. He rubbed his hands with satisfaction as he watched the effect of his eloquence on their faces.

I too looked at my audience. Everything was as I wanted it to be. I was on the verge of rubbing my hands with satisfaction too, like the Sheikh, when I happened to glance at Abou Ebeid and saw his silly grin was still on his face. I made one last bid to throw him in the shade. I

went on to tell them how bored I had grown with the
long holiday and how I longed to practise dissection again.
And to show them how serious I was I declared I was
ready to pay as much as five pounds for a body, if only I
could lay my hands on one.

I walked away with my head high that night and Abou
Ebeid saw me to the door saying, 'Go in safety, my Bey.'

I never gave another thought to the things I said that
night. I forgot all about them and the 'rigor mortis' business
and the iron scourges with the prongs. It was all small-talk
one was bound to make where there was company and I
thought no more about it.

One night, shortly after, I awoke to the sound of furious
barking in front of our door until I thought the dogs were
chasing Azrael himself. Then I heard a knock. It did not
alarm me as we were used to having people knock on our
door at all hours on account of someone being taken with
sudden colics, or a case of retained urine. My father was
the only one to be annoyed by the disturbance. It made
him curse the day he sent me to medical school. He always
feared that I should go out in the night to see a patient
and get killed by someone lying in wait. Why anyone should
want to kill me was a question my father never asked himself.

I opened the door to find a man standing before me
bending under a huge load he was carrying on his back.

'Evening, Doctor.'

The voice was familiar, but I couldn't distinguish the
face although it was the small hours of the morning and
the light of day was beginning to come through.

'Who is it?' I asked.

'It's Saleh.'

'The Sphinx?'

'That's right, Doctor, I've been knocking nearly an hour.
The dogs almost tore me to pieces. Here, make way.'

I stepped back a little to let him in. He put the load
down on the ground.

'The goods,' he said.

'What goods?' I asked, peering into his face.

In the dim light I could see only that he was smiling. That was the first time I ever saw him smile and I realized there must be more in the matter than appeared at first.

He told me he was on his way back to his little hamlet, after having sat up rather late in the town, when he saw a body floating in the stream. His heart turned over with joy for that was exactly what he had been looking for. So he went and fished it out and laid it on the bank until he ran to Abou Shendi's house and begged him to lend him some sacking which he promised to return, forfeiting his wheat. He ran back to the stream and crammed the body into the sack, and carried it through the cornfields to avoid being seen, until he reached our house.

Dumbfounded, I tried to follow his account, staring at his enormous bulk and his swollen eyes, while I suffocated with the stench rising from the sack. Suddenly I found myself barking all sorts of abuse at him.

He waited until I finished before he spoke again.

'Easy now, Doctor. Any wish of yours is a command. This is the least I can do for you. It's not as if I'm keen on the five pounds. I'll take anything you give.'

I barked at him to take the damned thing back wherever he got it from.

He waited again until I finished then he blinked.

'Don't upset yourself so, Doctor, I'm not a greedy man, I'll settle for one pound.'

I flared up again.

'Are you mad, man? Have you gone completely out of your head?'

He made a sign of impatience.

'Alright, I'll come down. I'll take twenty piastres. Come on, same as if it were only an arm.'

At long last, after my voice had risen to a roar, and he could see from my face that my fury was genuine, he was able to realize I wasn't haggling and that I meant what I said about his taking the body back immediately. His face

froze and he resumed his usual grim expression, shutting
his eyes.

'Is that a proper way to treat me, Doctor? Do Effendis
tell lies? Did you or did you not say a body was worth five
pounds? Would you swear on the Koran that you didn't?
Would you?'

There followed a long argument where I insisted I
remembered nothing of the kind and where he repeated
everything I had said word for word giving proof and
evidence. I couldn't persuade him to return the body as
my growing embarrassment was making me falter. But
when I saw he was adamant I threatened to inform the
Omdah. His face darkened at that and he looked on the
point of a tremendous explosion.

'This is no way to treat me,' he broke out. 'No indeed.
After all, it's you who asked for it, and now you say you'll
go and report me. I'm not taking it back, I tell you. I swear
by my father's head, I'm not. You can do what you like.'

The shouting must have awakened my father, for now
he was coming out of his room.

'What's going on?' he asked.

I hurried up to him, and tried to explain there was
nothing, only a case of colic, but it was too late. He had
already spotted Saleh standing in the doorway with a
face that augured nothing good.

'What does this boy want here? He's a thief.' To all
landowners all fellahin are thieves. 'He'll filch the kohl
right off your eye, he will. He and his father before him.
What brings you here at this hour, boy?'

As he said this, Father was walking towards Saleh who
was still standing in the doorway. I couldn't do anything
about what happened next. Father stumbled on the sack
and nearly fell on his face, wondering angrily what had
brought the thing there and what had brought Saleh.

'What's this?' he asked, feeling the bundle with his
hands. 'Have you been stealing water-melon, you son of a
bitch? And why should you bring it here, hey? Hey?
What's the doctor got to do with water-melon?' Then,

'Well, for heaven's sake!' he exclaimed with a shock. 'That's not water-melon! What's that stink, boy? Well, for heaven's sake! For heaven's sake!' My father was shouting uncontrollably. I had never seen him so terrified before. Saleh and I rushed up to steady him in time before he fell over. I led him back to his bed. He was speechless with shock. But it only lasted a few minutes. He sat listening to me, utterly flabbergasted, as I told him the whole story. He kept shaking his head unable to believe it.

'The thief!' he kept repeating, 'the Goddamned thief and son of a thief!'

When I returned to the Sphinx I found him sitting on the ground with his back to the wall and his head hanging down. He was obviously very upset. He stood up when he saw me.

'I say, Doctor, anything wrong with the gentleman? It's all my fault! Oh my God, why did I do it?' he moaned.

I was just preparing the dressing down I intended to give him when he spared me the trouble.

'Believe me, Doctor. I never swear by my father's head in vain,' he said, bending to check the cord that tied the sack. 'But I will make an exception for your father's sake. I am so ashamed of myself. The devil be damned! What got into my head? I was going back home in peace, why did I not mind my own business? Moris rigo indeed! What's that got to do with me? But then I'd thought to myself, "The doctor will take you in with open arms, boy, you can count on that." Well, as I told you, I never swore by my father's head in vain, but this time never mind. . . .'

He stood the bundle up.

'Here, Doctor, give me a hand. Mind your clothes. Here goes,' and he hauled it up onto his shoulders with fantastic strength.

'Never mind, Saleh, I'll make it up to you,' I blurted, quite tongue-tied.

'That's alright,' he said as he turned, his bundle turning with him. 'It's only a bundle after all. Can't be worse than that scourge the Sheikh was talking about. Only a bundle, no worse than what I'm used to carrying.'

He went out of the door and had nearly disappeared in the dark when he suddenly stopped and turned to face me.

'Only try to remember, Doctor. By the Prophet, and your conscience and all that's holy, did you or did you not say you were looking for a body?'

The Dregs of the City

I

It is almost impossible for a person to lose his wrist-watch, because usually if one takes it off one keeps it in a place that is safe and if one has it on, the strap, or whatever contraption keeps it in place, is so firm that even a skilled pickpocket can do nothing with it. That's why it must be a strange feeling for a man to turn his wrist in order to know the time and find his watch missing. 'Must have left it somewhere,' he says to himself and soon remembers where, because there aren't many places where one's likely to leave a wrist-watch lying about. That's what happened to the judge.

In the middle of a court session boredom drove him to want to know the time and when he turned his wrist, his watch wasn't there. And while the lawyer for the defence was pleading the cause for the defendant, Judge Abdallah was mentally reviewing all the places where he could have left his watch. Perhaps on the dresser in the bedroom, but he couldn't be sure. Better ask Farghali. Farghali was the court janitor, and asking Farghali was the first thing that occurred to him when something went wrong. If he couldn't find his pen, Farghali would look for it; if he mislaid a file, Farghali would know where to find it; and when he had a headache, Farghali was the first to know. Dismissing the court was no problem. All he had to do was stand up and give the order. So when the lawyer for the defence paused for breath, he saw his chance and immediately ordered the court dismissed. Everyone stood up, the puzzled attorneys wondering whether the lawyer's force of language had anything to do with the adjournment, or whether it was simply in order to investigate the law on work contracts more thoroughly.

Back in his room Judge Abdallah was about to ring for
Farghali when he looked up and found Farghali already
there, all of his fifty years in an upright column of bland
obsequiousness. His stomach politely pulled in, his tarboosh
leaning to the right so that the tassel came exactly over his
right ear, he was leaning forward ready to catch every
word.

'Yes, sir,' he said in a tone which years of servility had
tempered to convey his submission and his perfect willing-
ness to carry out orders.

The tassel of his tarboosh shook violently as Farghali
denied knowing anything about the watch. Quite the
answer Judge Abdallah expected since he knew Farghali
couldn't possibly have seen his watch, but he had to ask
him from sheer habit.

Probably on the dresser in the bedroom, he mused again,
and the first thing he did when he got home was to look
for it there. He was annoyed not to find it. Some inner
pessimism, which has a habit of surfacing at such times,
made him suspect the watch had been stolen. He had to
make sure, just the same, so he began to search the draw-
ers, and the bedside table, and inside the wardrobe, and
under his writing table. He turned the house upside down
to no effect. He had partly undressed meanwhile, keeping
on only his shirt, socks and shoes so he could bend and
stretch more easily in order to reach all the places that
came to his mind, only to find cobwebs and heaps of dust.

He sat down to think, crossing one bare leg over the
other. It annoyed him to have the even flow of his life –
dull and monotonous as it was – disturbed by this petty
incident. The disappearance of his watch from a room
with four solid walls vexed him, as he could find no
reasonable explanation for it. He was nagged by the usual
sense of loss one can't help feeling for even the most
trivial objects. This watch for instance was worth nothing
in itself, and only the fact that he had lost it enhanced its
value. It was neither platinum nor gold. Just a plain

fifteen-stone Ancre he had bought before the war and
which had stayed with him ever since. In fact it gave him
a good deal of trouble as it frequently broke down and
the cost of repairing it had come to exceed by far its
original price. He didn't particularly care for it. Nevertheless, it annoyed him to part with it. Had he flung it out
of the window himself he would probably not have felt a
pang of regret. But losing it in this fashion irritated him
in spite of himself. He didn't care about its material value.
He was well off, and money had never been a problem to
him. He was born and raised in easy circumstances. Even
when he was a student at law school he had his own
Topolino. His father was alive then, and he was used to
spending lavishly.

For a bachelor, his flat was furnished quite luxuriously
but that did not mean he was a rich man. Just average.
In fact everything about him was average. If one were to
pick a hundred men at random from all over the world
and consider their height and weight and the colour of
their skin, the result would be something like Judge
Abdallah. There were no extremes about him. Even with
his tea. 'How many lumps?' Mrs Shendi would ask as she
poured his tea. And then she'd remember. 'Oh, I know.
You like it just right. One and a half.' 'You know me,
madam,' he'd say, looking up from his game of bridge,
'moderate, that's what I am.'

Speaking of bridge and Mrs Shendi, it shouldn't be
imagined he had made a habit of going there. In this too
he was moderate. His calls were neither too frequent nor
too scarce. Just enough to sustain a cordial relationship. In
this respect, like in all others, he was a gentleman. A gentleman with a fixed smile he reserved for strangers. And he
never took the lead in getting familiar. He spoke little and
with reserve. And since life treats people according to
what they are, it treated Judge Abdallah moderately,
neither raising him suddenly nor suddenly pulling him
down. He proceeded evenly from law school to the office
of public prosecutor, and from there to the bar, just as he

had planned it, and his father before him.

So that such an event as losing his watch was bound to cause a ripple.

He needed a cigarette to help him sort things out. He was not a smoker but he kept cigarettes in his desk for visitors. Occasionally, he didn't mind a puff. He got up now to light one, then came back to his place and crossed his legs. He realized then that he was practically naked. He got up again and slipped on his pyjamas before anyone saw him. Not that anyone was likely to. Being a bachelor he lived alone. He did intend to marry, of course, but not before he turned thirty-five. He was thirty-two now which left him a margin of three years. The reason he had decided to marry at thirty-five was that this would be midway in his life-span, as he had reckoned he'd live to be seventy or so like his father who died at that age and his grandfather before him. There was nothing foolish about that. Many people make serious decisions in their lives based on groundless intuitions that do not stand close scrutiny.

He sat on the rocking chair beside the big wireless set. By now he had definitely eliminated the possibility of Ga'afari stealing the watch. Ga'afari was above suspicion. He had been in the family for generations, one of the many things bequeathed to Abdallah. He was a good man, naïve and loyal and wholly devoted to his master. One of those people who not only accept their destiny but look upon it with awe and reverence. The 'master' was to him a being apart whose needs were sacred. He had been with him in the house at El Mounira and when he moved to his present flat in El Gabalaya Street he moved down with him. He lived in, and that made him a bit of a nuisance sometimes.

Ga'afari was honest and neat in his work and he hardly spoke a word all day, which suited Abdallah as he particularly disliked idle talk. But he had found him in the way once, two years before, when he wanted to bring a girl to the flat and the presence of Ga'afari had made it awkward. He could not bring himself to walk into the flat with a girl, under the eye of that old servant who had been a witness of the family's past glories, and who had known his father and his mother and raised him from childhood. And yet he felt it was time he had a fling. Time was fleeting, he was past thirty and his years of freedom were slipping by with nothing to show for them.

With regard to women in his private life, his conduct was exemplary. Not because he considered 'such things' improper or from any moral scruples, but simply on account of a bad experience he couldn't forget. He had picked up a girl once when he was a student, together with a friend of his, and they had taken her in his friend's big car on the desert road to Alexandria. The next thing he knew was the appearance of certain alarming symptoms which, though they were treated promptly and with good results, made him vow not to come near a woman again except in wedlock. Ever since, as far as he was concerned, a woman was only a microbe with lipstick and nylon stockings, dangerous to contact. This could have induced him to marry but he stuck to his plan. Meanwhile he was nearing the deadline and his life was as arid of women as the barren desert. This state of affairs became intolerable and he decided suddenly it was time he put an end to it. That's when he began to urge Ga'afari to get married himself, and actively helped him find a wife. After that he informed Ga'afari he would not be needing him the whole day, he was free to go after lunch. All in order to clear the flat so he could be free to make the best of his remaining bachelor days.

Once Ga'afari was out of the way he intended to have the flat teeming with women, without really knowing how he was going to set about it. When he found that with or without Ga'afari things remained pretty much as they were, he was forced to give more thought to the matter. For many years he'd had little to do with women until this sudden obsession got hold of him to the point that he was prepared to overlook the microbe business. But where was he to find a woman?

In the meantime he had become a judge and although
he was only a young man he had to be careful of his
reputation and the dignity of his post. Nor could he con-
fide in anyone. His immediate circle were all starchy
officials in high posts. Hardly the sort of people he
could be intimate with. As for his old friends from student
days, his small car was one reason why he didn't have
many, and even those had gone their own way. When by
chance he happened to run into one of them they would
be off to an effusive start full of hearty back-slapping and
well-old-boy-where-have-you-been and it's-great-to-see-you,
after which they would discover that that's about all they
had to say to each other besides a passing remark on the
good old days and the professor with the funny face.

So much for his male acquaintances. As for the females,
he simply had no connections to speak of. There were a
few relatives, some of whom he detested. Some were rather
attractive and those intimidated him. They were either
married or in pursuit of marriage, and they all had their
eyes on him, having labelled him a prize catch. But he had
a positive aversion to marrying a relative for no reason he
could explain even to himself. He took care to keep out of
their way, as the slightest motion on his part could be mis-
interpreted and he had no intention of finding himself
caught in the end with a wedding ring.

Then there was Mrs Shendi for variety, a fifty-year-old
widow, passionately fond of bridge, who had a salon which
attracted high officials of the state. She had a gift for conversation, and for smiling understandingly and listening
to people's troubles. Her complexion was rather dark which
suggested she came from the heart of Upper Egypt although
she insisted she was of Turkish origin.

Many of her visitors were married women who were bold
and emancipated. He enjoyed talking to them. Occasionally he would comment on a new hair-style or an elegant
pair of shoes, but it never went beyond that. He was
painfully aware of his shortcomings. He knew his appear-

ance was not particularly impressive and that his conversation was uninteresting. All he ever managed to convey were dull platitudes which people suffered out of deference for the word 'judge' appended to his name. That's why it never occurred to him to embark on anything more intimate with the ladies of Mrs Shendi's salon. He lacked the experience and besides they made him feel clumsy.

He cast about elsewhere. One girl abused him roundly. Another gladly accepted his invitation to the pictures and dinner afterwards at the Auberge. But when his hand happened to brush hers, she stood up and walked out in a virtuous huff.

His sweeping obsession led him to try Mrs Shendi herself. Her response was lukewarm. She gave in to him in an offhand manner and treated him like a naughty boy. For days afterwards he couldn't live down his mortification or get over the fact that she was a woman of fifty and that his behaviour was unbecoming for a man in his position.

Still, he did not give up. That was how he got to bring Nana to the flat six months after he started dating her. That had been a trying business because it had to be done on the quiet. It was the high cost of dating for a man in his position. He could only take her to places on the outskirts of Cairo, which he had to scout for himself first to make sure he was not likely to run into anyone he knew. And all the time they were together he would be on edge, relaxing only when she said, 'Bye, bye,' and squeezed his hand as he dropped her off.

It was quite a triumph for him when he got her to come to the flat, although his timidity did not allow him to go very far with her. He knew she was having him only because she wasn't a top-ranking beauty, and she knew it, too. Still, they managed to develop a relationship which ebbed and flowed until timidity wore off, and resistance weakened, and he developed a certain feeling for her that made him seriously consider marriage. She was pleasant, she came from a good family, and she shared his interest in law. Only the fact that it didn't take much to get her

into the flat rather put him off. And the feeling nagged
him without cease until he gave up the idea altogether.
But he had learned a good deal in the meantime. Intimacy
with one woman is revealing of the mechanics of all the
others. Soon he mastered the kind of talk they love to hear.
He developed an expert eye for fashion, and a knack for
catching subtle details and half-tones of colour. He acquired
other skills as well. Flashes of wit, the glib rejoinder, the
double-edged quip. And the open invitation couched in a
smile, and the look that carried a world of meaning. Suddenly he'd made it and he found himself with more than
one girl to his credit. One for going to the movies with, one
to teach him dancing, and so on. They came and they went.

One night at a nightclub he was introduced to a group
which to his surprise, included more than one member of
the judiciary. He was also introduced to an entertainer,
or more precisely it was she who had introduced herself,
and he pulled out his wallet and treated her to an expensive
drink, and she insisted on opening the door to his flat herself as they returned, both a little tipsy, later that night.

No, it was definitely not Ga'afari who had stolen the
watch.

II

It must be Shohrat.

Judge Abdallah was thrilled to find himself involved in a
situation which absorbed him so completely. It was more
than he could keep to himself. All those suppositions and
assumptions storming through his brain had to be shared
with someone. He had to have Sharaf.

He got up and dialled the Actors' Syndicate. The number
was engaged but he kept on trying, hardly able to wait.
Sharaf was the only person in the world he wanted just
now. This was a thing to be discussed only with Sharaf.
He must be at the Actors' Syndicate. He had to find the
scoundrel.

Sharaf and he had been friends since the days of El Mounira when Abdallah lived in the big family house. Sharaf lived in El Mounira too, but he came from a poorer background. That's why Judge Abdallah felt relaxed and at ease in his company. It was easy to speak his mind with Sharaf. He could tell him things he could never tell his rich friends and relatives; that's why he cared for Sharaf more than he cared for any of them even though Sharaf was by no means an important person. He had dropped out of school at an early age and drifted from one job to another for a while before he took up acting, for which he had always had a liking. He took a job acting on the radio. All his parts were short. His longest role consisted of only three words. In spite of that he was very proud of himself as an actor. He even had his own views on acting and the theatre and life in general. His permanent residence was at the Actors' Syndicate.

Theirs was a peculiar relationship in spite of their affection for each other. Judge Abdallah was a busy man but there were days when he found himself with nothing to do and the world would stretch before him yawning into infinity. It was then that he remembered Sharaf. He would ring him at the Actors' Syndicate. That was the only call Sharaf ever got from anyone. 'Come along, Shafshaf,' he'd say. That's what he called him. Without asking who was calling Sharaf would immediately head for El Gabalaya Street, sometimes by tram but more often on foot, and climb up to the elegant flat in one of the tall buildings overlooking the Nile. There would be iced water, and food, and conserves, and sometimes beer and an easy chair where he would recline to act his part.

His part was to listen. Listen to his friend Abdallah talk. And when Sharaf and Abdallah talked it was mostly about Abdallah. There are few people one can talk to about one-self without their interrupting to speak of themselves in turn. Sharaf was one of those. Abdallah would unload, droning on and on, sparing no detail, while Sharaf listened with infinite patience. He had made an art of listening to

Abdallah, taking care never to appear bored or impatient, or to draw on his cigarette and shake his head mechanically, pretending to follow what was being said. He gave his full attention, his eyes shining as the situation developed, smiling when a smile was required, and coming in on time with a laugh. He made one feel he was truly concerned about one's welfare. It was not uncommon to find a listener like Sharaf, but then one knew it was only to oblige. Sharaf was not like that. He showed real concern. He asked questions, he argued, he wanted details. It was a comfort to talk to Sharaf for there were moments when he saw himself as a trivial being, a person of no consequence, particularly when he was surrounded by people whose talk was alive and witty, which made him feel miserably inadequate. With Sharaf he could let himself go, speaking with force and eloquence. He could be entertaining and witty and full of wisdom as Sharaf himself proved when he made him stop to repeat things he had said which particularly pleased Sharaf. Like the listeners to a Koran chanter who would ask for the repetition of verses by which they were particularly moved. Very often he wished he could get his wise sayings to Sharaf on tape just to show his friends there was nothing wrong with him. If anyone was wanting it was they.

Sometimes in his conversation Abdallah would express his private views on life and what he thought about people. Generally when a person is asked for his opinion on a certain matter in the presence of others he will say only what is conventional, out of deference perhaps, or fear of being different, or simply to avoid an argument where he could be the loser. Few people have strong personal convictions, and fewer still make them known or have the courage to uphold them. And rarest of all are those who combine courage and the power to convince, not only upholding their convictions but converting others to them. Still, the fact remains that each one of us is wise within limits, and that it is not given to all to preach their wisdom to others.

Like everyone else Abdallah had come to form his own
convictions which he derived from his own experience.
But those were revealed only to Sharaf. The strange thing
was that of the two, Sharaf was the one to take them
seriously, Abdallah being more inclined to follow others.
It takes a good deal of guts to uphold one's beliefs.

Just then Sharaf walked in.

He was tall and gaunt with elongated features and an
untidy mop of hair. He immediately gave the impression
he was an 'artist'. He had a bashful smile and when he
smiled he revealed a protruding set of teeth which nobody
noticed. He went straight to the kitchen, as usual, and
returned with a glass of iced water which he started to
sip slowly. He removed his jacket and hung it on the back
of his chair. Then he sat down and crossed his legs as he
took the cigarette Abdallah offered him. Abdallah watched
him impatiently until he settled down. Sharaf was quite
aware of that and he took his time deliberately. At last
he spoke, fixing Abdallah with his eyes, trying to guess
what was on his mind this time. Was he feeling lonely?
Or was it a new love affair, or some new theory on the
development of crime in juveniles?

'Well, what is it?'

'The damnedest thing!'

'You've been promoted.'

'No. Shohrat stole my watch.'

'Shohrat who, the dancer?'

Shohrat was not a dancer, or another friend of Nana's,
or anything to do with that category of women. Shohrat
was Farghali's gift to Abdallah.

It all began with one of Abdallah's periodic rebellions
against his thwarted attempts to improve his love-life. So
far all the women he got to know, in one way or another,
succeeded only in making him feel inadequate. He could
never relax in the presence of Nana or any of the others.
He had always to be considerate, always ready with sweet
talk, always prompt with a smile that must never fade. To
make up for his inadequacy he doubled his efforts to

please while not one of them ever bothered to please him,
until he got quite fed up with the lot of them and decided
to try other channels. There was no reason why he
shouldn't.

Next day he called Farghali and began to complain to
him about the problem of domestic help. Men servants
were dishonest. Elderly women were tiresome and too frail
for work. Farghali bowed his head. He agreed with every
word. Another time Abdallah appeared very annoyed and
told Farghali he had just sacked the new servant. Farghali
was extremely sorry and cursed all servants, this one in
particular who certainly deserved all that was being heaped
on his head. A third time, Abdallah spelled it right out
and asked Farghali if he knew of a good honest woman
who would work for him. She must not be too young, he
was careful to stress. Farghali bowed again, he quite agreed.
Abdallah appeared to be thinking. On second thoughts, he
added, it would be better if she were not too old. Middle-
aged, sort of. Farghali bowed once more. That was best,
of course. But Abdallah changed his mind. It would be
better if she were a young person after all, who could deal
with the household chores, particularly as the back stairs
were steep. The flat was on the seventh floor. Farghali
bowed again, with a smile this time. He understood perfectly. He promised to fill those requirements by tomorrow,
Friday.

It was three o'clock in the afternoon when the bell rang.
Ga'afari had gone, having cleared up after lunch. Judge
Abdallah opened the door himself. Farghali's smile filled
the doorway. He had a habit of smiling with his eyes shut
when he was pleased about something. Evidently he was
very pleased now. He was out of uniform, wearing a plain
suit, no doubt the gift of some previous official. Old and
worn and several sizes too big, it had obviously never once
known contact with an iron. His shirt looked more like a
nightdress and his tie had eroded from wear to the thick-
ness of a string.

'The goods are here, sir,' said Farghali.

'Where?'

'Come along, Shohrat,' he called.

Shohrat came in. Abdallah did not look at her immediately. He felt embarrassed, and worried that the neighbours might have seen her going in. She stood in the corner near the door of the living-room. He called Farghali to his study and asked him to sit down. Farghali absolutely refused but obeyed when Abdallah insisted. Abdallah was slightly annoyed at that as he suspected there a degree of familiarity he should not have encouraged. His mind went back to the woman. He was curious to see her face so he got up and went back to the living-room while Farghali stood sharply at attention. He gave her a furtive look so as not to make her feel she was being inspected. But he found it hard to keep his eyes off her. She was not what he had imagined. What he saw was a plain, native woman of the people like thousands of others. The sort of woman who is made to be a wife and a mother. Hardly the type for a servant. He couldn't quite place her; nor could he make up his mind whether she was plain or attractive. Anyhow, he thought, she would do. He went back to Farghali and asked him what her wages would be. Farghali refused to go into anything so vulgar. He could give her what he pleased, he said, if he were satisfied, if not, there were plenty of others. Although Abdallah was not too pleased with this arrangement he gave him a cigarette. The next thing was to get rid of him, so he gave him a fifty-piastre tip which Farghali was quick to pocket in spite of voluble protests.

After he had gone Abdallah returned to the study and sat down. The woman was still standing in the living-room. 'Come here,' he called.

She came, still wrapped in her *melaya*. She stood leaning on the open door. Abdallah gave her another close look. He was quick to sense a seductive female under her strong features and her ruddy complexion.

'Your name is Effat?' he asked, deliberately distorting her name.

'Your servant, Shohrat,' she replied.

There was a feminine ring to her voice that caught his ear, and he noticed that the way she said 'your servant' was more by way of courtesy than humility.

'Are you married?'

'Yes.'

'Children?'

'Two girls and a boy.'

He was still looking at her, searching for that thing experience had taught him to look for in a woman, which revealed how far she was willing to go. It wasn't there. He noticed she was still holding her *melaya*.

'Have you had lunch?' he asked. It was three o'clock in the afternoon.

'Yes, God be thanked,' she said, her eyes on the floor.

Which meant she hadn't. He suspected she'd had no breakfast either. He told her to go to the kitchen where there was some food left over. She mumbled something about really having eaten. But he insisted and when he saw she did not know the way to the kitchen he got up and showed her. He returned to the study and sat thinking. She was not what he had expected. There was power in that woman. She was poor and wore a *melaya* but there was an air of dignity about her that women of her class seldom possessed. Perhaps it was the purity of her features. Would he dare, he wondered. Her kind was not easy to beat down.

When he heard her moving about in the kitchen he guessed she must have finished eating. He went and stood at the kitchen door.

'Have you worked before?' he asked, as a way of starting a conversation.

'No. This is the first time.'

Ah. He'd heard that one before. The lady of quality fallen on bad days. That was an old trick. He didn't want the conversation to end there so he ordered her to remove her *melaya*. She obeyed and stood looking for some place to put it. The kitchen was bright and sparkling and she dared not put it down there. Finally she laid it on the edge of the rug in the living-room. She was wearing a very faded silk dress underneath.

'Can you make coffee?' he asked with a cunning smile.

'Sugar?' The expression on her face was quite candid.

'Yes, and make one for yourself too,' he added on an impulse.

'Thank you,' she replied as she started on it.

Somehow he felt disturbed. For some reason he was aware that this woman Shohrat could see through him. He felt she knew what was in the back of his mind. Why he had spoken to Farghali, and why he was standing there now putting himself in her way? She was probably laughing at him. It only made him more determined. Suppose she were – suppose she did see through him, what then?

She was standing before the stove, her eyes fixed on the coffee pot, or at least so it seemed. He came and stood behind her.

'Where do you live?' he asked, placing a hand on her shoulder, not troubling to listen to what she replied, for what he really wanted to know was how much she responded to the touch of his hand. He felt her stiffen and he moved closer, defying her resistance. She quivered and drew slightly away as he held her more firmly to prevent her moving.

'Where are the cups?'

Beads of sweat clustered on his forehead and his throat went dry. Sharply he ordered her to clean the flat after she was through with the coffee, and then he went back to his study. She brought him the coffee there and stood respectfully before him, her eyes looking down.

Almost immediately she started to clean up. The rugs were rolled back and the chairs moved out of the way and the tile floors were flooded with water. Abdallah was watching her movements as she bent to scrub. From the back her legs were a pinkish white, and the mounds of living flesh that rubbed against the threadbare fabric of her dress called out to him with maddening insistence.

He went and stood near her pretending he was supervising her work, giving her orders. There's dust in that corner. Over there too. Bend over so you can reach it better. Her eyes were on the floor and her whole body was exposed to his gaze.

When she finished she asked if there was anything more to be done. There wasn't. She asked what time she should come next day. Half past two in the afternoon. That suited him best as Ga'afari left at two. For a moment he was tempted to have another go at her but decided to put it off for fear of another rebuff. She wrapped herself in her *melaya* and walked demurely out of the room.

When the door closed behind her Judge Abdallah cursed himself for a fool. To let a woman like that brush him off. A woman who had walked into his flat of her own free will and when nothing stood in his way. A full-blooded male in his position given the slip by a two-bit slut like her!

III

She came regularly now, every day at half past two. Every day he thought of trying and every day he put it off. Until one day she was rearranging his bed as he had ordered her (for Ga'afari usually made it in the morning) when he suddenly came upon her and took her in his arms. She struggled hard to break free, begging him to let her go. He paid no attention and after a long struggle she was forced to give in. He was thrilled when he felt her resistance collapse, even though he wasn't sure whether she was overcome by his physical strength or by sheer despair. He let her go and she ceased to struggle. What was the use now?

He went back to her after a while, curious to see her reaction after what had happened. He was annoyed to find her eyes were red and her cheeks flushed.

'What's the matter?' he asked gruffly, expecting her to

mumble as usual something like 'nothing', but he got no reply.

'What's the matter? What's eating you?' he asked again, but still she said nothing.

'I asked you what's the matter,' he repeated sharply, shaking her impatiently.

'I've never done it before,' she said slowly and the tears began to roll down her cheeks.

He refused to believe it. This imperious woman was staging an act she had probably played many times before. Did she take him for a fool or was she angling for a raise? But she never asked for a raise. And when she spoke to him after that she avoided his eyes, either looking down or busying herself with something.

He was quite satisfied with her. The best part of the experience was that her capitulation was his own achievement. It was neither his money, nor his position, nor his manner that did it but the sheer power he could exercise over her. His triumph had brought an end to the hidden struggle between her inflexibility and his weakness, for he had always known that of the two she had the upper hand. Had she been one of the ladies of Mrs Shendi's salon and not a servant he would never have dared to go near her.

The next time he also met with resistance but it was the resistance of one who had despaired of resisting. They always got off to a stormy beginning which slowly resolved into the tranquillity of habit. Her presence in the flat was a novel experience. The sound of her step, or her appearance in the doorway, her *melaya* wound tightly round her body, aroused him, and he'd find himself considering whether to have her right now or whether it would be better tomorrow. What impression was he making on her? How did he perform as a lover? He'd have her now, or maybe after lunch. He was troubled and restless. The familiar noises of the household, plates clattering in the kitchen, the broom brushing over the rugs, or her voice coming from another room, textured, modulated, provok-

ing, fell on his ears with special impact. It was an exciting
adventure which had all the ardours of expectation and
all the thrills of surprise. But seldom does anything withstand the strain of habit. What was once the source of
boundless joy would one day hardly cause a flutter.

His greatest hurdle at the beginning was to break her
down, but once that stage was over all he had to do to get
her to bed was to squeeze her hand, or smile out of the
corner of his mouth, or simply ask her about her 'health'.
Then she would try to elude him, and he would chase her
round the flat, and what had started in jest would turn
into a sweeping want that had to be answered right away.
When she sensed his desire she'd start to shift about; a
pale smile would form on her lips, a blend of reserve, indifference and a good deal of submission. But the moment
he was through with her the smile became ironic with
undertones of contempt.

When the novelty wore off and habit settled in he took
to giving himself up to her with complete abandon. He
omitted the niceties and he treated her as little more than
a live mattress on which he sprawled and stretched and
tossed and turned and relaxed without restraint. And when
habit dulled the edge of excitement he began to look for
new thrills. He began to whisper obscenities which he
wanted her to repeat to him. Brutally and deliberately he
would lay bare the most hidden reaches of her soul, even
the things a professional whore would still want to keep
private.

It took him a long time to realize she had not lied.
He really was the only man to have had her besides her
husband. If words did not convince him he was convinced
by his daily observations, and by her spontaneous reactions,
and the vague intimations by which the truth is always
known.

One day he asked, in another attempt to probe into her
being, 'Do you love me, Shohrat?'

The question sprang from an overriding need to know.
What made this woman with children and a husband, who

came to him from want, this woman whom he had seduced and whom he could have any time he wanted, what made her accept this situation? Was it only because being her master he had the upper hand, or did she want him for his own sake, for the male that he was?

The question preyed on his mind. He longed, if only once in his life, for a woman to desire him, any woman at all, even if it were only Shohrat. He was continually looking for evidence that she was that woman, but there was none. She was still pleased when he let her keep the change from the housekeeping money. Sometimes she would ask for a loan of ten or twenty piastres. He couldn't tell if she really needed them or if that was her way of getting what she could out of him. Nor could he tell if she was doing her best to please him for his own sake or as part of her duties as a domestic. Nothing pointed to anything definite, he could not see clear on that score because his awareness of Shohrat was confined only to the limits of his desire for her.

Meanwhile life went on as usual : work, law-suits, preambles long overdue, bridge, Mrs Shendi, dates with other girls, drives in the car, and a hundred other things that made up the fabric of his life. Questions pounded in his head only at the instant when he desired Shohrat, otherwise he dismissed them.

Shohrat did not answer his question immediately. She looked down as she always did when he spoke to her.

'I asked you something,' he said, pressing her closer.

'Does anyone who loves another ever admit it?' The simplicity of her reply moved him. It was direct and candid which made it impossible to doubt its sincerity. It made him wonder how a woman so untutored could reason with such clarity. Had she been educated he would have suspected she was repeating something she had read in a book.

'Of course, he must,' he said to draw her out a little more.

'Then he would not be saying the truth.'

'What do you mean?'

'Love is in the heart. What is spoken aloud is not love.'

What did this woman know of love? What did it mean
to her? He had read what scholars had written about it.
He had discussions with his friends concerning it, people
of his own background. Now he had a rare chance of
picking the brain of a woman who had no experience of
love.

'Tell me,' he asked, 'what's this thing, love?'

'How would I know?'

He pressed her to say more.

'How am I to know? It's love this, and love that; that's
all you hear all the time,' she said impatiently.

'But you, what do you say?'

'I say it comes from God.'

'What do you mean, from God?'

'I mean one loves only if it is the will of God.'

'But what is the meaning of love? How does it make
you feel? What do you want when you love?'

'Oh, come off it.'

And she would go no further. Not because she could not
find an answer but because she could not bring herself to
say what she wanted to say.

What begins as fun sometimes suddenly takes an unexpected
turn and ends in earnest, like this discussion with Shohrat.
It raised a new issue. He did not know her husband. He
did not even remember whether his name was Saleh or
Mahmoud although he had asked her once. Nor did he
know what he did for a living. All he knew was that he
had sired her three children and that for this reason there
must be something between them. What was it? He wanted
to know only because he had placed himself between them.
He had to know which of them she loved better.

'Who do you love better, me or your husband?' he asked
her bluntly one day as they lay in bed. He was sorry the
moment the question was out and would have changed
the subject had he not been so keen to know the answer.

He was vexed when she said nothing. She just looked

down and smiled. What did that mean? Surely she would
have told him if it was him she loved better. Suddenly he
was filled with a childish fury. The slut. What did she see
in a man who could not even support her? Should he sack
her and put an end to this issue? But he knew he was not
up to facing the consequences. She had become a habit
with him. She knew his ways and catered to his needs and
he rather enjoyed the pleasant rut of his life with her. And
then there was that irresistible pull she had on him. Perhaps it was a question of time. After all, she had spent
years with her husband and only a few days with him. He
would teach her how to love him, that destitute creature
with a *melaya*, he would teach her yet. It became an
obsession. How to subjugate this woman, how to dominate
her.

His anger kept mounting until he thought he would
burst.

He did not burst. An hour later he was sitting in his
study submerged in the files of forty law-suits that were
coming up before him in the morning. He had forgotten
all about Shohrat and her husband and when he ordered
her to make him tea it was in the same tone as he ordered
Farghali to call in a witness.

IV

When it started, the affair with Shohrat was a solemn
experience. When he called her it was in answer to a
compelling urge; and when she came every nerve in his
body awakened to her presence. But it wasn't long before
it all fizzled out into dull routine. Nothing in her stirred
him any more. Her body was nothing but a piece of
property he could throw on the scrap heap any time. He
felt elated when he remembered how he had succeeded in
breaking her resistance. He was the master and that's all
that mattered. Shohrat did not count one way or another.
She could be another of those bits of bric-à-brac cluttering

his flat for all he cared. And yet he was often nudged by the doubt that he had not scored a real victory. He was not certain of that victory. Did he fully possess her? Did he dominate her to the extent of overshadowing her husband?

On the whole he didn't really care whether he possessed her completely or whether she still belonged to another. But there were moments when his vanity clamoured for assurance. He decided to cut down her salary and see what happened. If she stayed on his question was answered and if she quit it was just as well.

Actually he had already begun to complain to Farghali whenever the latter asked fawningly how things were going. He would scowl and start to list her faults. She was sloppy, she was lazy, and it was time he tried someone new.

When at the beginning of the month he handed her her salary minus one pound, she took it without a word and put it in her small faded wallet, her face crimson. Next day when she didn't turn up he felt a pang of remorse but he had no intention of tormenting himself on her account and he decided to ask Farghali to find him another servant. But he never got round to doing that as something more pressing had cropped up unexpectedly. Coming out of the cinema one night he happened to catch a glimpse of Nana with a young man. Investigations led him to discover she was having an affair with him which vividly reminded him of his own interlude with her. For quite a while he could think of nothing but to get her back.

Three or four days later when he was parking the car in the garage in the basement on his return from work he noticed Shohrat, wrapped in her *melaya*, squatting on the floor near the door. It annoyed him and he decided to ignore her, so he went up through the little back door connecting the basement with the front entrance to the building. But just as he expected, the bell rang in his flat a few minutes after he went in. It was Shohrat. He gave her a pale smile and let her come in. She didn't speak. Nor did he know what to say to her. He watched her in-differently as she went to the kitchen and removed her *melaya* in order to start work. He sat in his study and called her. Although a shy man by nature, he was not shy of Shohrat any more. She was perhaps the only person he knew of whom he was not shy.

'Well?' he asked.

'I had to come back,' she said looking at her wet fingers.

'Then why did you leave in the first place? Was it the money?'

He couldn't help the bitterness he felt as he said this, for he remembered that the money had been his way of testing her attachment and that he had failed the test.

'My little girl was ill. I had to take her to hospital.'

He could see through the lie. Nevertheless he felt a little pity. Perhaps it was her paleness. Her face was drab and sallow. Humility made her features droop, and it looked as if that was her pride seeping out with the sweat that was dripping from her brow.

'Isn't three pounds enough for you?'

'I'm not saying anything, only Moneim has quit his job.'

'Who's Moneim?'

'My husband.'

'Oh. And why did he quit?'

'They say they're retrenching or something.'

'What does he do?'

'He's a tanner.'

'Where?'

'In a tannery, somewhere near the slaughterhouse.'

He muttered something but made no comment. Suddenly he was filled with a loathing not directed at anyone in particular. The more he looked at her pallid face, and those moist beads on her forehead, and her submission, and the more he thought of her children and her jobless husband, the more the hatred and revulsion grew. The idea of her husband's profession brought up revolting visions of dirty hides, and the stink of cattle and glue, and Shohrat's embraces and his bed.

'Alright, go,' he roared at her. She turned and went.

He cursed himself afterwards for having started this

conversation. It gave him no end of a headache. Where
before Shohrat hardly opened her mouth, now she never
stopped complaining. One day it would be about her
husband. He had found a job in a dairy. Next day he had
quit the job. Then it was her daughter. She had fever and
diarrhoea. Next her daughter was dead. And then the
landlady. She was harassing them for the rent. There
was no end to her tales and he had brought it all on himself. She had become a nuisance and he simply had to get
rid of her. But he lacked the nerve. He was also human.
He could not bring himself to sack her when he knew she
was in such hardship. There was nothing but to put up
with her – but even that had a limit, and no sooner would
she start complaining than he would quickly shut her up.
On the other hand he was still a man, and she was still
that woman who had appealed to him once. And his flesh
was weak even though at times he was put off by the
thought of her husband's profession.

One day he heard her suddenly laugh out loud. A long,
unrestrained peal that startled him. For in spite of what
there was between them she knew her place, and he had
a good deal of consideration for her which she herself
inspired. She was not given to levity. That's why it alarmed
him when he heard her laugh that way. It was coarse and
vulgar, very unlike her.

'Shohrat !' he called.

'Yes.'

He thought he suspected a hint of coquetry there. When
she came he found he did not know what he wanted to
say or why he had called her, so he asked her if she'd got
rid of the cockroach he had seen in the kitchen.

'I found him cuddling up to a female roach,' she said
with a giggle. And she laughed again, loud and shrill. He
stared at her, amazed. The expression on her face was
new. It was no longer that of the plain good woman who
was a wife and a mother he had known at the beginning.
Her cheeks were sunk, and round her eyes there were
incriminating shadows. Even her smile was no longer the

candid smile it used to be, but an artful grimace, full of affectation. He was appalled.

He kept worrying. Had he done that to her? Was he the one who had made a whore out of that simple married woman? He knew in his heart that he was, but he wasn't going to be bothered by qualms of conscience. A man feels remorse only when he is afraid of punishment. Abdallah had no punishment to fear. What he feared was the new suspicion that gnawed at him night and day. Was he alone to blame for what had happened to Shohrat or was she carrying on with others? The doubt made him mad with jealousy. The jealousy of a master over his slave not that of a lover over his beloved. The mere thought that she should put him on a level with some errand boy or a mean mechanic was unbearable.

From now on he regarded her with suspicion. If she went out shopping he would question her closely when she returned. Where had she been? Whom did she see? Sometimes he would hear her laughing all the way up the stairs. As soon as she was inside the door he had to know why and with whom she was laughing. And he never let the slightest offence pass without comment.

The change was amazing. Before, she never dared raise her eyes when she spoke to him. Now she looked him in the face and muttered if he scolded. The former gentle soul became a hard, nagging, irritable creature. She argued and answered him back word for word. He cursed himself for his weakness. What made him put up with her?

The fact was that the more her hold on him grew, the weaker he became. Very often he could not keep up his side of an argument. Almost as if there was something in her that he dreaded. Did he fear for his reputation if she chose to speak? Should things come to a confrontation he knew he would not be equal to her brand of logic, sound and irrefutable where his arguments were based on assumptions and delusions derived from his obsession with her conduct.

Strangely, he met her arrogance with compliance. Sometimes he even played up to her in subtle ways like affecting concern for her family. That husband of hers puzzled him. She never stopped complaining about him, lamenting the day she had agreed to share his life, cursing his apathy and his indolence. But somehow it was all on the surface, as if she didn't mean what she said. Some days he was employed, but more often he was not, while she continued at her job. The children were her favourite topic. It was she who had to answer for everything to everybody, she told him, even to their landlord and her husband's current employer. Sometimes he worked in the slaughterhouse, sometimes he delivered cheese from door to door. Sometimes he made coffee in a coffee-shop, and sometimes she herself would prepare the mixture for the bean rissoles which he fried and sold at their street corner. He never lasted more than a couple of days at any one job which made Judge Abdallah marvel at this family, forever hanging on the brink of destitution, wondering how they would have managed had Shohrat not been working for him. He was full of compassion for them, just as he would be for the victims of an earthquake in some distant corner of the earth. It was only compassion, however, and it was soon dispelled by the boredom inspired by Shohrat and the tiresome problems of her family.

One day around the middle of the month she came asking him to lend her a pound. It was no coincidence that it was the day after he had gone to bed with her.

'What for?' he asked, a little irritated.

'Oh, just a loan,' she replied wantonly, looking at him boldly which so unnerved him that he gave her the money. This was her last month with him, he decided firmly.

'When will you return it?'

'I'll pay it back by instalments,' she answered and followed this remark with a ripple of laughter that made him shudder.

A few days later he was astonished to see her come for the first time without her *melaya*. She was wearing a new skirt made of a cheap checked material, and on top of that she wore an old rag which with a little indulgence could pass for a blouse. Her head was uncovered and her lips were painted a faint red, probably with a red pencil. She was repulsive to look at.

'What are you all rigged up like that for?'

'I'm ashamed of my *melaya* in this building. Isn't this better?' she added over her shoulder as she took a few steps forward and turned to display herself, looking at him boldly. He turned down his lip.

'And what does your husband say?'

She exploded an air bubble in her chewing-gum before she replied.

'Don't ask me.'

'Why? Where's he gone?'

'Over at the café. He's been sitting there for three months.'

'Why?'

'Out of work,' she said with a stream of laughter. She strolled across to the mirror and looked at herself this way and that. 'Well now, don't you think I look much better like this?' she asked.

He vowed to himself she must go at the end of the month. She stuck her hips on one side and passed her hand languidly in front of her face with a dramatic gesture.

'Don't you think I'd do well in the movies?' she asked as she stood striking poses in front of the mirror.

'They all say I should go into pictures,' she said again, when she got no answer, as though in reply to herself.

V

The following day she turned up in her *melaya*. He asked sarcastically what had happened. Nothing. Her old blouse wouldn't do any more, she had to have a new one. She had the material but needed a pound to pay the seamstress. This time he was certainly not giving her even one millieme.

He couldn't figure out her new attitude. Whatever lay behind it portended nothing good.

He often wondered what she did after she left him. Probably walked the streets. *Melaya*-clad women were cheap. Perhaps with a skirt and a blouse she could raise her price. He was almost certain his guess was right but that wasn't his business. He was finished with Shohrat anyway. A few more days and he would tell her to go for good. She could do what she liked.

When she came the next day she asked for the pound again, saying the blouse was ready. But he wouldn't let her have it. She had borrowed enough as it was and he never expected to see his money again. Besides, he had quite made up his mind she was going. He wouldn't wait until the end of the month. He'd tell her tomorrow.

That's what he told himself every day. And every day he forgot. He had every intention of doing it as he left the flat every morning. He would go down to the garage and walk round his car to make sure it had been properly cleaned. He was certain every time to find reason to reprove the garage boy. Then he'd drive down to the court which would start to come to life with his arrival. Greetings from right and left, people shuttling to and fro, moving up and down. And Farghali, no sooner would he see the car coming than he'd scuttle downstairs, all in a fluster, to open the door and bow and take his briefcase, trotting behind him at a respectful distance. In the waiting-room he would take a quick look at a couple of cases that were shortly coming up before him, and which he had put off considering several times before for lack of time. Then the old clerk would come in, with his spectacles and his slow movements which were even more depressing than his spectacles. It took him five minutes to say good morning, and he'd hang around forever. Then coffee, and rushing madly through the files as the hands of the clock drew near to ten and the people got impatient outside in the court-room, and he heard their protests grow steadily louder. Then he'd rise and take his seat in the

court-room as the sound of Farghali's voice calling the
court to order made the ceiling rise like an arch of triumph.

For a while he would concentrate on the cases that
followed one another in quick succession. Then his attention would start to wander, and he'd fixe his gaze on the
face of some witness which he found repellent or on a
lawyer who irritated him. And then he'd start playing with
the idea of resigning from the government and setting up
a private practice.

And so the day would come to an end, and the car would
take him back to the garage where he'd park it and go up.
As soon as he'd opened the door and seen Shohrat's *melaya*
lying on the floor like a black banner, he would remember
he must speak to Farghali about firing her. He would speak
to him in the morning.

But in the morning too, he would forget.

VI

This, then, was the story he told Sharaf. It was all very
clear. Shohrat stole the watch in order to sell it and pay for
her blouse since he had refused to lend her the money.
She had probably also guessed his intention of firing her.
Sharaf was listening, stretched in his chair, limp and
lethargic. Judge Abdallah was irritated : he had expected
more from his friend than this cool response. He felt Sharaf
had let him down, leaving him to deal with the situation
on his own. The impudence of the woman; a mean low-
down servant, to dare to steal his watch knowing that
sooner or later he would find her out. That was not just
impudence but an insult. That shameless woman was daring
him, but he was going to show her, he was shouting now
to Sharaf. She won't get away with it. He wasn't going to
let her make a monkey out of him.

They sat thinking what to do, Sharaf sprawled in his
chair, and Abdallah pacing the floor. It was Sunday,
Shohrat's day off. That had been a new arrangement. It

had been introduced when Abdallah had begun to tire of
Shohrat, and he'd started to nibble around for variety. He
reverted to the old game in order to clear the flat for other
visitors.

The obvious thing to do was call the police, but on
second thoughts it was better not to. For one thing the
police have seldom been known to trouble about petty
thefts. What's more, once it gets known that the police
are on the track, stolen things have a habit of disappearing
into the bowels of the earth. Besides if he informed the
police, he would have to answer a lot of questions which
were better left alone. He did not trust Shohrat not to reveal
their real relationship which could damage his reputation.
So there was no question of the police.

Farghali, then. After all, it was he who had brought
her, on his responsibility. He must be told what had happened and it was his duty to recover the watch. But Sharaf
pointed out that Shohrat might not be as as naïve as she
seemed; she might not give in so easily in the first round.
And then curiosity might lead Farghali to pry too closely
into his private affairs. It would be more prudent if Abdallah were to handle the matter himself, the better to keep
things under control.

The problem was how to reach Shohrat at this time of
day when neither of them knew where she lived. Farghali
was the only one who knew her house, and neither of them
knew where he lived either. If they waited till the next day
there was no guarantee that the watch would still be waiting. It had to be now. She must be taken by surprise if
they hoped to recover the watch. So Farghali had to be
found. Abdallah remembered he had been in the same
situation once before when he had left his keys with
Farghali and the latter had to be summoned after hours.
He remembered now, it was the garage boy who had found
him.

He called the porter and ordered him to send up the boy
immediately. He paced the floor until the bell rang and the
garage boy came in followed by the huge black porter. He

was only a young boy, peasant-like and in rags. He was fairly dark and obviously a runaway from his native village. It took Judge Abdallah a good five minutes to make the boy coherent, so frightened was he at being summoned by a judge, and overawed by the luxury where he stood and all those eyes fixed upon him. At first he denied any knowledge of Farghali. But under the pressure of a cigarette and many assurances that he would come to no harm, which Sharaf and the porter sustained, his memory returned and he volunteered to find Farghali. The porter was immediately given a pound and told to get into a taxi with the boy and not to return without Farghali.

While awaiting Farghali, Abdallah sat down to lay out the strategy. Suppose Shohrat were found and he were to face her, would he trust himself, when before, he, her master, had never been able to stare her down? He didn't allow the thought to linger; in his present mood he felt able to stare down a whole battalion of Shohrats and wrench from her not only his watch but her very guts. If she insisted on denying it he would threaten her with the police. But to get her properly rattled he needed to dangle a policeman before her eyes. He knew a young adjutant from the second precinct at Giza, a pleasant young man who might be willing to co-operate. But on the other hand if the young man refused, Abdallah would have exposed his private life unnecessarily.

Suddenly he had a great idea. Sharaf. Who else? Sharaf could be made to play the part. Sharaf was a little taken aback at first but gradually the idea began to appeal to him. He got up and went to the mirror and tried a few grimaces in rehearsal. He was going to enjoy this. He went back and announced to Abdallah that he was accepting the part. Abdallah cheered and his laughter, buoyed by his irritation, rang loud and hollow as Sharaf continued to fool about, ruffling his hair, making faces and striking attitudes, warming to his part.

The bell rang and when the door was opened Farghali stood panting in the doorway. The porter had refused to

let him use the lift and had dragged him all the way up the
back stairs. Farghali was wearing his usual old over-sized
suit and his dark tarboosh, slanting on one side, while
sweat poured out of his face. No sooner was he told what
had happened than he recoiled in horror. 'The damned
bitch! The damned bitch!' he kept repeating, all the way
downstairs, and until they got into the car.

Abdallah sat at the wheel with Sharaf at his side and
Farghali on the edge of the back seat almost standing on
tip-toe had the roof of the car allowed him. He muttered
and swore. He would show her, he promised. He'd bring
ruin on her house. He'd make orphans of her children.
He'd get her hounded out of the neighbourhood. She'd see.
He kept talking of the 'neighbourhood' as though it were a
place known to all, and when Abdallah asked him where
that would be he answered promptly, 'Right next to El
Roum Lane.' And when again Abdallah asked where that
would be he named places neither he nor Sharaf had
ever heard of. Finally, it turned out that the 'neighbourhood' was a blind alley somewhere behind the mosque of
Al Azhar.

VII

Abdallah was elated as he started off on his quest for
Shohrat. It was a novel and thrilling adventure not only
because he was certain to recover his stolen watch but
because it was going to prove his perspicacity. He looked
forward to tracking Shohrat down, to catching her red-
handed, to watching her reaction, observing her fear, her
denial. New complications would surely crop up but he
would know how to handle them. He could already see
himself later, telling his friends how adroitly he had
handled the whole affair. For the moment he refused to
consider adverse possibilities even though they crowded in
his mind. He was weary of thinking and debating and
making new plans every time he discovered a leak, and

from that moment he decided to shut off his mind to everything but the scene unfolding before him.

He felt himself melting into the landscape as he rolled along. He could not remember the exact moment when it happened or any specific incident that relegated Shohrat to the back of his mind. He could only recall the dim beginning from El Gabalaya Street. The long, clean, shaded street; the open spaces and the tall stylish buildings. The peace and the quiet, except for the noiseless flow of elegant cars and a few pedestrians. The air was serene and the Nile flowed gently, and the car glided along as though on a carpet of silk. And Sharaf beside him smoking in silence, smiling with amusement when he remembered his part. Farghali was in the back, holding on to the front seat, the car reeking with his smell, spluttering into Abdallah's right ear every time he spoke.

At the bridgehead they are joined by streams of cars pouring from Zamalek and Gezira and Dokki and Quizeh. Bright, colourful, shining, like flocks of birds. In the whirlpool of Kasr el Nil Square their ranks are swelled by shabby cars and taxi-cabs before they diverge to other streets where movement never stops; narrower, with closer buildings, noisier, with more pedestrians. At Ataba it becomes one great merry-go-round. Automobiles and buses and tram-cars and pedestrians and horse-drawn carts mill around in utter chaos. It reaches a peak when they turn into Al Azhar Street. Here, it is a madhouse of pedestrians and automobiles, screeching wheels, howling claxons, the whistles of bus conductors and roaring motors. Policemen blow their whistles, and hawkers yell in the blistering heat. The roads and pavements are a moving mass of flesh. Everything is wholesale. Riding a vehicle, trading, and even accidents come wholesale. From time to time a warning to be careful rises above the din like the last cry of a drowning corpse.

Driving becomes an agony under volleys of abuse from pedestrians and the eloquent retaliations of Farghali, and Abdallah's determination to get even with Shohrat and avenge his wounded pride. He would strangle her willingly. Get his fingers round her neck and press, tighter and tighter. He is pressing the claxon which lets out a hoot that falls noiselessly on the enormous crowds. Traffic goes at a crawling pace, exasperating, maddening. The mosque of Al Azhar rises indomitable on the skyline, behind a haze of dust. It has stood for generations, watching the deadly struggle while it has remained constant, insusceptible to change. Then they turn to the right.

Acting on Farghali's advice they park the car and do the last leg on foot. A few paces and Abdallah begins to feel hollow as though he had been left alone in an ancient deserted place. The noise dies down, the quiet is almost tangible. He is Egyptian through and through. His father came from El Mounira and his mother from Abbassieh. He has poor relations in Upper Egypt. He has travelled a good deal, gone to many places, and seen the extremes of poverty. Yet here was Cairo, and this place where he finds himself is part of it. The incredible scenes unfolding before his eyes amaze him beyond belief as he delves further in as though he were sinking in a bottomless pit.

The streets are long and broad at first, carrying illustrious names. They are macadamed and they have a pavement. There are crowded dwellings on both sides but they have numbers and terraces and decorated gates and the windows have panes and shutters. The shops have owners and tools and assistants and elegantly written signs. The people are clean-shaven and healthy looking. Their clothes are neat and colourful and well cut. Language is polite. The smell of burning fuel and fabrics and perfume fills the air.

The deeper inside, the narrower the streets. The houses shrink and shed their numbers. Windows have no shutters. Shops give way to stalls where the proprietor is himself the assistant and his bare hands his tools. Faces are paler and darker. Clothes are old and faded. Language degenerates into abuse, and the air carries the smell of spices and leather and glue and sawdust.

Still they continue, and the streets grow narrower until they become mere lanes with names that jar on the ear. Rough blocks of stone take the place of macadam and there is no pavement. Aeons of time separate the dilapidated dwellings from modern times, the windows are narrow slits with iron bars. There is less movement, stalls are few and far between. Features are coarse, faces are darker and beards begin to sprout. There is less clothing. No shirts with the trousers, no underpants with the *gallabieh*. Language breaks down to a jargon of grunts, and kitchen smells ride on the air. Still they continue and the winding lanes lead to alleys paved with dirt, covered with filth and water and slime. There are no stalls; goods are displayed on push carts or a showcase nailed to the wall. The houses have shed their coating of paint and the iron bars on the windows. Children and flies swarm in abundance. Features are coarse and swollen as though bitten by wasps. Clothes are threadbare, some are unclothed; language is loud and shrill, and the smell of slime and decay falls like a pall on the dismal scene.

As they keep on towards their destination the winding lanes and alleys lead to a place without substance where everything melts into everything else. The raised ground, compounded of years of accumulated dirt, welds with the dilapidated buildings groaning with age. The slimy ground is the same colour as the dusty walls. The smell of the earth mingles with the smell of humanity, and the low broken murmurs mix with the barking of dogs and the creaking of old gates, and the dead slow movement of inanimate creatures. The low grimy dwellings are a continuation of the graveyard, stretching forward as far as the eye can see. And the obsequious Farghali leads the way, a grave expression on his face, befitting the grave situation. People greet him and he answers curtly. They all know him and ask how he is getting on. They treat him with deference, him, the mean janitor, while back in El Gabalaya Street nobody knows the all-powerful judge.

They walk on through the crumbling buildings propped, like the people, against one another for support. The old lean on the young, the children lead the blind, and the walls support the sick. All are strung together like the beads of a rosary. One spirit inhabiting many bodies. Time does not exist. The child suckling at its mother's breast is the same one who crawls on the garbage heaps, and the same one girt with talismans against the evil eye. He is the child who died and the child who escaped death. He is the apprentice at the workshop, the one who fools around imitating actors and calling abuse. He is the youth in overalls drawing on the stub of a cigarette. The one with a job or out of work. He is that one near the wall, crazed with opium and Seconal and unemployment. He is the old man who prays all day calling benedictions on the children, lamenting the past as he paints himself a glowing picture of the world to come.

And the betrothed bride. She is the children's mother with the coloured head-cloth or the black veil. She is the beating mother and the beaten wife. She is that one rummaging for food to feed the hungry brood.

Farghali's voice comes dimly to Abdallah. He is pointing at the only upright building in the lane saying proudly it is his house, insisting they go in, not forgetting to curse Shohrat who is the cause of his disgrace. Abdallah asks where the blind alley is and whether Shohrat's house is still far. Farghali replies that they have almost reached it. They walk on, followed by inquisitive looks. And behind every suspicious look the word 'stranger' forms, implying danger and distrust.

The women at their doorsteps are weaving conversation out of their idleness. They lean their heads together as they watch the strange procession. The whisper travels from doorstep to doorstep. 'Police,' some say in a hoarse whisper. 'Health authorities,' hope the optimistic. Then they recognize Farghali, and their whispers die down.

And children. Scores upon scores gather in front and behind and on either side, their eyes bleary with ophthalmia and trachoma, and misery looks out of their haggard faces. Swarms of flies come in their wake. One child shouts as he hurls a stone at Farghali who reproves him mildly. Soon it is a game. The children gather round Farghali who chases after them and they scamper away with the flies behind them. Soon they come back and resume their game as the flies resume their buzzing.

Farghali is not sure which is Shohrat's house. He asks one of the women sitting at their doors who points to a house not far off. The name is carried from mouth to mouth, collecting conjecture as it travels. The women leave their places to join the procession of children. Their black veils and the dirt ground and the shouting of the children and the low mumble of adults are all one. The earth boils under the hot sunshine and the stench from its bowels escapes to the sky.

Farghali and Sharaf, surrounded by the curious crowd, wait at the door while Abdallah goes up alone. The house is dark. The interior is like the mouth of a toothless hag. Matches won't light and they drop to the slimy floor. Shohrat is on the second floor, at least that's what they said. The first floor is pitch black and the stink is foul; an army of rats seems to have gnawed at the decaying walls streaked with traces of brine and leakage. Dank, mouldy, as if just emerging from a flood. A woman washing at the door of a room in the entrance, one bare white leg exposed, stares at him with suspicion. Her hands stiffen; she can neither let go of the washing nor cover her bare leg. The stairs are worn and shaky, its wooden steps rotten and missing in places. His shoe creaks, and he is panicky with the danger of falling. For the hundredth time the light from the match is blown out by a dank breeze blowing from an invisible source. A cool dank breeze that chills his marrow, while outside the sun burns hot. The second floor can hardly be called a floor. A bare framework like the ribs of a skeleton forms the roof. Old tottering sloping walls, and a door on the landing. It is made of old rough un-polished wood, greyish blue, smudged with the remains

of dried-up dough, the excreta of birds and animals, and
the bloody imprint of a human palm, flanked by the drawing of a face like a witch's, chalked by some child.

He stretches a hesitant hand to knock on the door.

'I want a word with you,' he says to the face that
appears in the doorway.

She pales beneath the look he pours on her like a
searchlight. Apprehension and fear look out of her eyes.
It's Shohrat. She greets him in a broken voice and opens
the door wider to let him in. She is wearing a man's old
gallabieh slit down the front. Her paleness has travelled to
her feet making her toenails white. He is embarrassed.
This trembling woman stole his watch. He was out for her
blood when he started on her trail, but now he wavers. He
stands debating whether to go on or to turn back. Having
come this far, he must go on.

'I want a word with you,' he says as he had planned.
But his tone is not as he had planned. She lets him in,
pale and apprehensive. She tries to hide her embarrassment
behind a wan smile. He plans his retreat as he enters. Anything might happen. She might scream for help; he might
be assaulted and robbed or killed. Three children emerge
from somewhere. A girl, ten years old, tall, dark, skinny,
with beady eyes and an expressionless face. Her hair is
black and shiny, exuding an odour of petrol, one plait
undone and a wooden comb planted in the crown of her
head. Two other children, a boy and a girl, or possibly
two girls or two boys. They cling to their mother's skirt.
Out of the dark, penetrating the smell of petrol, four
pairs of eyes are fixed on him with mistrust. He swallows.

'I want a word with you,' he repeats mechanically.
Shohrat comes to abruptly as though in response to a
stimulant.

She sends the children away and shuts the door, but
they linger behind it, their eyes shining through the cracks
like glow-worms. His head is spinning. The room is close
and narrow. A faint light filters through a window high in
the wall. A decrepit four-poster, rusted all over, with a

grubby mattress. A coarse moth-eaten sack full of something is propped against the wall. A rabbit is sitting on it. At the other end is another grubby mattress, and empty tin cans and chips of wood and a miscellany of junk lie scattered about. There is a picture of the Imam Ali on the wall. He is shown smiting an infidel with his sword, but the infidel is still sitting upright in his saddle, his feet firmly in the stirrups, in spite of the gash in his head. Something stirs on the mattress : a man, tall and dark and bald as the water cooler standing beside him. He is stretched out with a scowl on his face, his belt unbuckled, with filthy underwear showing through his open trousers.

'I want a word with you,' for the third time.

'Yes?' Faintly with a tremor.

'Where is the watch?'

She stiffens and beats her breast with indignation. She denies with the fluttering of her eyelids and the increasing paleness of her face. He repeats his question. She repeats her denial. Intuition assures him she is the thief and he returns more vehemently to the attack. She tries to reply and the words die on her lips. He shouts and she cowers, holding on desperately to her pride. The screams of the children rise above theirs. The eldest tries to take them away as she hears what is being said to her mother. Scenting danger they refuse to go and leave her alone.

His anger grows and he threatens her with the police. He is at the door. She appears not to believe him so he goes to the door. It creaks open. Then he takes her to the window and they both lean out. 'Alright, Officer,' he calls and Sharaf replies with a wink. Abdallah's face remains frozen and he pulls Shohrat back inside. 'Hand it over or you get a year in jail.' She stumbles on her way. 'Think of your children.' She stops dead in her tracks at the word 'children' so he batters her again with more stress on 'the children'.

There are no tears in her eyes. The sleeping man turns and groans as he dreams. Shohrat calls out to him but he sleeps on in despair. Abdallah's anger grows and he repeats

his threat while something inside him whispers : this mother
is fighting for the entity of her family.

And his anger rises, giving his face a fearful mask, and
he makes a final threat, and her eyes look into his. There
is not a grain of pity in them, nor is there a grain of cruelty
in his heart. He does not know why he threatens, why he
persists, why he has no mercy, nor why he is not more
ruthless. 'You can search,' she says, and he knows she is
guilty. He kicks things over with his foot. The sack is full
of dry corn cobs. Under the bed there is an old wooden
doll and old rags and the smell of mildew. A pile of worn
shoes in a blanket of dust beside an iron tube. The cupboard is one metre wide, painted brown under a thick coat
of grime. Inside, a dead roach and a boiled potato, two
onions and a sealed packet of salt. Looking below, his eyes
shine as he starts identifying some of his belongings. Decorated candy boxes, a wooden box with inlay, red pencils,
lead pencils, the top of a fountain pen, part of an old
lighter. 'For the children, to play with,' Shohrat explains.
Also an old mended sock. A deep sense of shame makes his
heart sink and the blood rise to his head. 'Hand it over,'
he hisses for the last time.

The husband stirs as he shoos away the flies with a
sleepy hand, and the voices of the children at the door
grow louder. Shohrat opens her mouth and then shuts it
again. Noises come from her throat and her hair is
dishevelled. She trembles inside the floating *gallabieh*, one
hand frozen on the other, and a distraught look in her eye.
There are moments when he comes to his senses and he
realizes he is putting on an act while this woman is standing bare in her misery. The powerful traits of her face
which once had brought him low have withered with her
suffering. There is no joy in victory. He is torn by many
factions.

The tears come. She has found her voice. 'Those things,
I found them, I swear. I was going to return them.' The
simpleton ! How could she cave in so soon. And he had
thought he was in for a long struggle.

She moves to the open cupboard and fumbles inside and comes up with a broken glass. She pokes two trembling fingers inside and pulls out his watch. She hands it over without looking up. Buckets of iced water are pouring on him. The storm quietens down and his heart feels like lead and the horrible putrid room becomes unbearable. The watch is shining brightly in his outstretched palm, and the sight of it fills him with a childish joy. He turns it over in his hand, shakes it, puts it to his ear. It is still running, pointing at the exact time. Four twenty-five. He must go.

At the top of the stairs as he starts to move, he suddenly slows down, gripped by a feeling that he has done wrong. He calls Shohrat who reappears, her little brood clinging to her dress. The eldest girl watches her mother, her face expressionless, her hands holding on to her undone plait. Abdallah hesitates then he asks Shohrat why she did it.

'My pay is too little. You refused to lend me . . .'
He asks her again.
'The blouse, I had to pay the seamstress.'
He presses her.
'I am ashamed to appear in a *melaya*.'
She doesn't weep though tears are falling from her eyes like rain from a cloudless sky. Her answers are vague. He wants to know why she didn't pawn the bed or sell it instead of stealing. Because it isn't their bed, and more tears stream down.

'Then whose bed is it?'
'Om Hanem's.'
'And who's Om Hanem?' She is the woman with whom they share the room.

A gruff voice from inside is asking with a big yawn what the matter is. She turns to answer as he steps aside to go downstairs in a hurry. Once in the open he takes a big gulp of fresh air and dashes forward unheeding of the crowd before the door. They follow him with their eyes. Large probing eyes that want to know what the gentle-

man has done to one of their own. Farghali presses him
with an ugly smile. 'Well?' he asks, but Abdallah pays no
heed and Farghali won't give up. He persists, relentlessly,
like the splutter from his mouth. The curiosity of the crowd
closes in on Abdallah like a ring of barbed wire. They
want to know. He pulls out the watch and straps it on his
wrist and he hears their murmurs grow to a rumble. The
news is starting to travel. The women huddle together
whispering, and they send their voices to the sky asking
God to protect them from evil. The men growl whilst the
children prattle and reports of the incident fly from casement to casement. Shohrat is being torn to pieces and
her mangled remains are tossed from mouth to mouth,
while she stands pale, silent, frightened, resigned and
helpless.

When he reaches his car it is like reaching a lifebuoy.
Sharaf is not there. He's washed his hands of the whole
affair, explains Farghali, he said he could stand it no
longer. Abdallah is not astonished, he expected that from
Sharaf. Farghali's profuse apologies alternating with threats
and menaces as though he counted himself responsible for
the whole universe, irritate him. He gets into his car and
presses the starter the same way he presses on his bad
conscience.

Once more the wide orderly streets come into view. Once
more the people are clean-shaven and well dressed and
their features are fine. He leaves the push-carts behind and
joins the fleet of taxi-cabs and buses and private cars. The
nightmare is over. The air is lighter, the world looks
brighter, everything smiles as he looks at the familiar surroundings of Kasr el Nil Square. Here a light breeze begins
to blow, bringing people back to life after the lethargic heat
of the day. The mighty river flows eternally under the
crowded bridge. The tall buildings on the horizon look
like pigeon houses. The city is breathtakingly beautiful.

When he reaches his flat he goes straight to the terrace
and throws himself in an armchair and tries once again to
sort out the events of the day.

VIII

During the interval nothing had changed. There was the same old study with the same old terrace overlooking the Nile, watching the shift of scenes. The glaring light of day was slowly fading as if an invisible hand were turning off the sun-disk. The city paled as the light faded. The rays of the sinking sun dazzled the eye as they broke on the window panes. The sky was tinged with red and, below, the city took on the evening hue of steel before it settled in nocturnal blackness. It was almost totally engulfed by the night except for the myriad lights speckled on the surface.

The terrace was alone to observe the scene. Judge Abdallah was far away, brooding, motionless, scanning the face of the sky. His thoughts were hovering round a spot, lost in the shadows, somewhere beyond the minaret of Al Azhar. From time to time the metallic sheen of his watch would flash before his sight, and a scathing sensation would gush like a haemorrhage, urging him to fling it away into the river.

But he never did. Nor did he sit up all night on the terrace. In the morning he was on his way to work as usual, accompanied by his customary headache. The watch was still on his wrist reminding him of that nightmare excursion. He would hold it up for all his friends to see before he started to tell them the story. He had to drop many details. When he came to the blind alley, the scathing sensation returned and he would gloss over some of the descriptions and move hurriedly to the next part.

He never allowed Farghali to speak to him of Shohrat. Nevertheless, he was not against picking up whatever news Farghali communicated. How she had turned bad, and got a reputation and styled herself Amira.

One day driving down Al Malika Street he slowed down as he happened to catch a glimpse of her standing at a bus-stop. She was obviously not waiting for the bus. Her lips

were painted with real lipstick, and she was wearing the
same skirt in which she used to come to work, but what
particularly caught his eye was the new blouse that matched
the skirt.

Did You Have to Turn on the Light, Li-Li?

It was a joke at the start. Perhaps it was a joke in the end too. Actually it was not a joke in the real sense, but an incident, rather, which happened to involve those fabricators of jokes who were past masters of the art. It was not the fact that all those people who normally go to bed at dawn should rise at that hour in order to pray, which was the joke, or the fact that for the first time in the annals of the quarter of Al Batiniyya – that den of opium, Seconal and hashish – the people answered the call to prayer which came from the minaret at the break of day.

Nor was there anything odd in their praying with their heads foggy with dope. Forgetting that they have already recited the *Fatihah* they recite it another time, but they forget the words and then they remember them in the middle of a prayer so they start all over again. The joke, actually, came just as they were about to end the prayer. The incident is still one of the cherished tales they are fond of recounting. People around there were drug addicts for the most part, reared in banter and humour, for whom jokes and anecdotes were a staple diet. No sooner would an incident occur than they would seize upon it, adding frills and embellishments until they made of it a fantastic epic to rival the best of their local lore.

Oddly enough, the first prostration had gone in perfect order, so had the second, and only the third prostration, the salutation, and the uttering of the words 'There is no god but God and Mohamed is the Prophet of God' remained to terminate the prayer.

'God is the greatest!' called the Imam as he kneeled for the third prostration. They all kneeled after him, albeit a

little awkwardly, their joints stiff from disuse as most of
them had not performed their prayers for longer than they
cared to admit. Ten long rows piously repeated 'God be
praised' three times, and waited for the final response from
the Imam to conclude the prayer. When that failed to come
on time some began to suspect their count was wrong. So
again, slowly, they repeated it, but still the response failed
to come. A few resigned themselves to waiting, only too
glad to rest, their dizzy heads still laden with dope, but
most began to wonder what had happened as it was becoming clear the situation was rather odd. Still, they were hopeful that the Sheikh would presently pronounce the words
'God is greatest' and all would be well. But the longer they
waited the more their suspicion was confirmed that they
were facing a crisis. All sorts of possibilities began to storm
through their bowed heads which none of them dared to
raise.[1] Had the Sheikh been suddenly taken ill? Or had he
passed out, or simply died? Or could it be some devil had
induced him to take a whiff of hash, and he was suffering
the consequences now? Yet in spite of these conjectures
they still expected the response to come and restore peace
to their minds which by now had gone on a wild rampage
in the realms of phantasy.

Exactly how long they waited no one was certain. According to some accounts it could have been two minutes or it
could have been two hours, that is, if one were to dis-
regard exaggerations which affirmed that the pause had
lasted until echoes of the noon call to prayer began to
reach them from Al Azhar. There are also those who insist
they are still kneeling up to this moment.

But what was certain even to the most befuddled was
that an unusual length of time had passed and that all
was not well with the Sheikh. He had certainly not pronounced the *takbeer* for which they were all waiting and
which would have put an end to their kneeling posture,

---

[1] According to religious law any wandering of the eyes, of the
mind, or any coughing or irregular motion will annul the prayer
and the worshipper must begin again.

and the snoring wheezing out of all those drooling jaws.

At this point each one of them found himself faced with a problem he had never encountered before. What exactly should he do now, and what do the laws of religion say with regard to a situation like this? If one of them were to move and raise his head, would that annul his prayer, and possibly that of the entire congregation? And would he alone take the blame? Being freshly-returned prodigals made them once again recall visions of a God who promised reward and punishment, wielding paradise and the bottomless pit of hell. To the newly repentant new transgression was more than they would want on their consciences.

But time was starting to weigh, and wicked thoughts began to assail them. Like scoffing for instance, not only at their predicament but at the thought of what might arise if the Sheikh had got it into his head to take a snooze or, even worse, he had simply dropped dead. They would probably have to remain in that posture till the following day, or possibly till doomsday before someone discovered them, as the mosque was not a place people around there were fond of frequenting, for merely to walk past it stirred the conscience. But they were afraid to dwell too long on their devilish thoughts or on the ridiculous situation they were in, since they were irreverent by nature, and they dared not succumb to impiety for fear of adding to their sins. Even the most optimistic were forced to admit that they were in a real predicament when the light of dawn began to break, and the wan light of the electric lamp slowly faded. It was pitch black when they had started to pray and now with daylight appearing no doubt remained that the prostration was uncommonly long. The sporadic sounds of coughing, growing increasingly more frequent, were the only signs of impatience with a situation which did not promise to end soon. It was impossible to know what had happened without raising their heads, and if they raised their heads they annulled the prayer. None was willing to take the lead and bring upon himself the opprobrium of such a deed. All were waiting for someone else to start. The blame would then be on him. There was a vast difference between the guilt of one who leads and one who merely follows. The prolonged prostration was becoming an undisputable fact and it lasted until it defeated all doubts and misgivings and any inclination to laugh at the matter.

And since there is no joke so far, and since the real laughs haven't started yet, let us leave them as they are, prostrate, each of them fearing to be the first to trespass.

For that's exactly how I left them. I, Sheikh Abdel Al, Imam of the Mosque of El Shabokshi, in the quarter of Al Batiniyya.

Did you have to turn on the light, Li-Li?

Yes, it is I. Glory to him who makes the night follow the day. Sleep is in my voice for I wake with the cries of the dawn. I am the climber of the dark spiral staircase of the minaret. I fear for my chest and for my voice from the morning dew. The cold invades my eyes and I shut them from habit. I know that my call to prayer falls on deaf ears. The Godly are few in this quarter, and the truly Godly prefer the mosque of Al Azhar, not far from here. It serves nothing to strain my voice for it is drowned by the amplifiers from the forest of minarets surrounding mine. My call is for myself, for I am content to know my voice has reached God; that He knows I call for the ordained prayers as He has ordered. I am content to know He forgives the people of these parts whether they sleep or they wake. For in sleep they shut their eyes on their wrongdoings and when they wake it is only to do wrong again. Perhaps it is providence that got me appointed to this mosque, endowed long ago by a Turk who had whipped and looted his way to fortune. By building a mosque and making his grave lie near the *Kiblah* he hoped to buy redemption. He believed that the people's prayers, generation after generation, would bring him nearer to paradise. Even paradise you want to reach on the backs of others, you Turk!

I am the new graduate from Al Azhar. I loved God from childhood, and of my own will linked my existence to His faith. I smile at those who imagine I entered the famous school in order to become a chanter of the Koran because God endowed me with a pleasing voice. That is not the reason why I chose to enter Al Azhar, nor why I started to learn the Koran when I was a boy. The reason goes beyond that. A call from God. . . . It had to do with my place in a universe where none but He deserves to live.

Did you have to turn on the light, Li-Li?

How dazzling was the light in the midst of total darkness. One lone lamp in one lone room on the roof which seemed to flood the whole of Al Batiniyya where it crouched like a deserted camp. The houses, old and crumbling, bulged with living beings. My flock, my burden, or more precisely my defeat. My defeat at attempting to awaken God in the hearts of those who wanted to forget His existence.

I struggled, and at the end of a week there was a spark that kindled hope. I struggled more. They cast aside their false promises and their voices began to rise. I pressed on. They came, threatening, their eyes sparking fire. Listen. We don't want a wet blanket around here. If you want to stay here, mind your own business or you'll get what you're looking for. Nevertheless, instinctively I knew they were good folk, that in their hearts they accepted God and that they sought Him. But in their lives there is no place for a total God. He must accept them as they are, they will worship Him in their own way or not at all. According to their brand of religion prayer was two prostrations every Friday, and although they fasted by day during Ramadan, from sunset to sunrise they fed on weed. No transgression there. Show me the text where it is prohibited. As for alms, the rich gave freely. Sometimes in kind, as the faith commands. The pilgrimage to Mecca was the crowning glory for big-time traffickers which allowed them at least to swear by the Prophet's grave when they made a deal. Five

people only have I barely won over, the rest had no faith
in me. I realized the fault was mine. Before I could lead
them I had to know them; I had to live their lives to
change their ways. I had to be of them so that they be of
me. Theirs was another language. They had other values,
and other concepts, and special keys that opened the door
to their pale. I went out to them, I sat in their cafés, I
visited their homes. I never frowned on their doings. My
heart was with them as I watched and listened, and slowly
came near.

Did this have to be, Li-Li?

It was ordained, whether it was she or another. I did not
know that purity to that extent was seductive, nor did it
occur to me that in spite of my devotion to God I was only
a youth of twenty-five. I am chaste. Happy. Even in this
quarter where the ancient residents, like the new, had
taken refuge from the world. Then as now they were fond
of meditating, except that now they dwell on levity while
those of old dwelled on the sublime which led to the foun-
tainhead : to God.

I did not comprehend except when the signs became
frequent, and unmistakable in spite of the purity of my
intentions. One day I happened to recite to them. They
liked my voice and they called me again. I knew then that I
had touched their hearts. The doors that until now were
shut in my face began to open. They wanted nothing of me
but my voice and my recitation. They rejected the preacher,
and the mentor, and the Imam; only my voice could draw
them where I wanted them to be. God in the abstract is
hard to conceive, so let the beginning be through His word.

The listeners who gathered round me were all men. I did
not know that they screened a larger audience of women.
The moment I began a recitation the rumour spread like
wildfire and in a flash they flocked down and came to listen,
sighing with every cadence. Trouble began. Every time I
went to the mosque I found a woman waiting for me.

Always with a question, or the pretext of one. But I never allowed my eyes to travel from the ground. Still, I was making headway. I had succeeded in getting them to pray and I was happy to see they were urging the men to do the same.

One day I was asked a question that rocked me to my bones. It was a young woman. Those feet upon which my gaze was fixed could only belong to a young woman. Faltering a little at first and then becoming more bold, she told me that for months her husband had deserted her bed; she tried everything to bring him back but nothing worked. His addiction was the cause. There was no hope of a cure and she feared the evil path. What was she to do?

Soon the questions became confessions. Master, I obeyed the devil and gave in to the delivery boy whom my husband sent with the vegetables. What shall I do? What shall I do, Master, for I saw you in a dream? What must I do, Master, when my brother comes stoned in the early hours and will not let up until I yield? Every night I yield. I want to repent. Will God accept repentance from the likes of me? I want to repent at your hands, Master.

There was no hint of repentance nor a shadow of restraint in the way she clung to my hand.

Satan.

These people had long and frequently given themselves up to him. For long years they had strayed in the paths of ruin and they knew no other. Satan. Around me and everywhere. In the woman's low whisper. In the look aimed at my back burning like a red-hot iron straight from the flames of hell. To face the devil without flinching I learned to master the bold stare and by that I lost the timidity which made of me the object of their lust. And with a withering look, I was able to stay their gallant approaches.

Did you have to turn on the light, Li-Li?

'My name is Li-Li, haven't you heard of me?'

A bold stare deflected my gaze where I looked. Natur-

ally, I had heard of her. She accounted for half the rumours
and gossip and all the contentions that kept the quarter
humming. Part-English, part-Egyptian, she was the wonder
of all time with her glossy red hair and honey-coloured
Egyptian eyes. Li-Li was the fruit of a week-old marriage
between her mother Badia and a British soldier called
Johnny. The morning after he spent the night with Badia,
unlike our shifty lads, instead of giving her the slip, the
dolt asked her to marry him. A week after they were
married he was called back to duty and she never saw him
again. He got killed in the war. To that short-lived union
Badia owed a monthly allowance she had never dreamed
of, which for twenty-five years she cashed in regularly at the
British Embassy. For the first time money ran freely
through her hands, which tempted her to run a small
business financing local small-time pushers.

It was there that Laila, as her mother called her, grew
up. Li-Li was the name her English grandparents gave her
when they came from England after the war to see their
grandchild. They tried by every means to get custody
of the infant but Badia clung stubbornly to her child.

She gave her an education in spite of the sundry characters going in and out of her flat where she chose to sit at
the door. Sometimes she sat in the doorway down in the
street, generously exposed and totally indifferent to what
people would say in a neighbourhood where she counted as
a rich woman, and where she ordered the men to run her
errands. She carried on openly with one or another without a qualm. But Li-Li, she would get an education. She'd
see her right through to the end. She'd make a lady of
Li-Li.

Educated or not the European is an enticing creature,
much more so when the heady wine of Egyptian blood
runs through her veins. Although she received an education
Li-Li did not learn. She was ambitious. Even as a child
she was aware that she was a cut above others. Even when
she served cheap drinks in seedy cabarets where she joined
foreign troupes, or when she haunted the offices of second-

rate impresarios. She never doubted that one day she'd be
a great lady, that she'd know fame and glory and that the
world would be at her feet.

'God be with you and light your way to the true path.'

'You light me the path and gain your reward from
heaven.'

'The light is in you. It must come from your heart.'

Did you have to turn on the light, Li-Li? Did you have
to?

'I want you to teach me to pray.'

'I have a book. You can have it.'

'I want you to teach me, privately.'

'God forbid that I should sin. Go, and may He forgive
you.'

One day the allowance stopped coming; the money
dried up; the mistress was ageing and ill health set in.
Li-Li's pitiful earnings were all that remained.

Many times I tried to avoid her but she stood in my
way wherever I went, her eyes like electric sparks flashing
from pole to pole, now Saxon now Egyptian, her devastating beauty beyond anyone's reach. They tried force, money,
crawling on their knees, but Li-Li gave herself only to
foreigners. That was the secret she revealed to no one. In
the end, as with all stubborn cases, they gave up and took her
as she was. They bowed to the fact that she belonged to no
one, and since she belonged to no one she belonged to them
all, for all to guard and protect; forbidden and desired.

Light.

A window of shining light.

I am blinded.

The light is near. Only across the narrow street. The
minaret is on a level with the window. I gazed inside. One
look swept me up like a whirlwind from the pit of som-
nolence to the peak of awareness. An awareness full of
terror, as I realized I was facing something wondrous and
overwhelming.

There is a high wooden bed in the room, what else besides I do not know. A woman is reclining on the bed, one leg slightly bent, her milk-white form half clad in a flimsy garment that barely covers her breast. It is the first time in my life that so much of a woman's flesh is revealed to my sight. I came round to myself half-way down the stairs gasping for breath as I fled. My terror turned to a sweeping fury.

I am caught in a snare.

I who came here to conquer the devil. My ambition dwindled until I am content merely to ward him off, to shun his abode, and beware of his many disguises. I find myself at the break of this day caught in a snare. I, who sought to defeat him in others, I run for fear he defeats me in myself. But my plea, you demon, is that you tracked me down when I did not know you existed.

How often was your wickedness engraved on our hearts until you came to be the image of evil. Not once have you been coupled with beauty, although that is where you love to lurk. In the shape of a woman, in the folds of luxury, or in the sweetness of a smile. That's where you hide your bait.

I went back upstairs.

What I saw I erased from my thoughts. The light from the window, the room, the street, the house, the whole area I blotted out of my mind. Let it be a war, a blazing raging war.

Oh, God! My cry sounded strange to my ears for that was not the sound of my voice. After the benedictions my call went up from my depths to the vault of heaven, sharp and shrill and endless. A powerful call that bore with it the frailty of mortals and all their limitations, as it reached out to the Omnipotent and Everlasting. But now it rose in a feeble gasp, shackled by my impotence, never to reach the heavens but to crash down from the minaret and perish on the ground.

My heart grows faint. I am afraid. Not of the devil but of myself. How often have I caught myself, too ardently lending an ear to those meretricious and lustful women. I cannot help the searching look in my eyes, nor can I ease the pangs of deprivation or the torments of my flesh.

Oh, God!

I was pure as the crystal fountain when I followed Your ways. Solitary, as though I were the only creature of Your hand. To gain acceptance I know I must go through the ordeal. So let it be a hard one.

I shall not flee.

I shall look and take my fill of her. The agony is past bearing. By allowing the lesser sin I shall triumph over the greater one.

It is she, Li-Li. The devil incarnate. Temptation in the flesh, tossing in her sleep, her body spilled on the bed, an incandescent glowing mass of flesh. There. There is her breast and there her belly. Her hair slides gently down to cover them. She turns and it slides back.

Oh, God! I cry for help. Not the cry of earth to the immensity above but my own desperate call as I sink. I continue to gaze for I cannot tear my eyes away. How evil is man. How evil I was to think I could conquer the devil alone. Alone I am nothing. My strength derives from God and what there is of Him in me.

Satan has me in his grip. My eyes he has riveted to Li-Li's white form, and with all his might he seeks to wrench from me my very soul. How little I knew the extent of my weakness.

Oh, God, who answers every prayer. All powerful God who knows my impotence. You who gives will to the slave, who knows my suffering, have mercy on me. Though I bear up I am defeated. I am horrified to discover at the crucial moment the frailty of what I believed to be my strength. Face to face with the devil, I know this is my battle for survival.

Oh God, will You leave me to fall? Will You have me err? Will You forsake me for Satan to rule and dominate. Help me my God, for I am in the abyss. Come to my aid for You are my only hope.

Why did you turn, Li-Li? Why did you let your flimsy covering fall away from your body, so dazzling white? So white that it shines with a light of its own. Stark naked, heaving and dashing, twisting and turning, your soft limbs languidly scattered at your sides. . . . What blazing hell is this that dwells in you which neither the rising dawn nor all the cold in the world can cool?

All in the glaring light.

Did you have to turn on that light, Li-Li?

It was not his loud voice that roused the people from their sleep for none of them could remember ever being roused from his torpid slumbers by a call to prayer. In truth it was an intimation of something marvellous and beautiful which called them from their beds. The voice was filtering through to their rooms like a heady perfume seeping into their sleepy nostrils; warm and tender like a melody in a dream. But they know they are not dreaming; they know they are thrilling to the stark reality of that voice.

Oh, God!

How often that call is uttered. In prayer and supplication; in sorrow and in gladness. How often did it come with the last breath of life and the first beats of existence. Uttered by the child, and the man, and the sinful, and the repentant. By the hopeful and the desperate wavering between hope and desolation.

All woke to that one call. Like a magnet it drew them out of their beds and into the streets with a feeling in their hearts they had not known before. A joyful feeling that they were close to God. A merciful God whom they had nearly reached.

They met in the mosque, the water from their ablutions hardly dry on their faces. Having never met before at such an hour or such a place they looked at one another like strangers meeting for the first time, their ears picking up the soothing strains of the call to prayer; food for their souls for when they shall hunger.

Presently, and in great confusion, they began to flock outside heading for the minaret to seek Sheikh Abdel Al. They needed to know whether the voice was truly his, whether it was truly of this earth or whether it flowed from heaven. So great was their rapture they did not realize that the Sheikh had come down without sending out the full call to prayer. Pale and sallow he descended from the minaret and with a sign of his hand stopped the rushing crowd. Immediately he went to the *Kiblah* and prepared to pray.

Yes, I prepared to pray for now I was worthy to pray.

Because I have triumphed I am worthy to pray. The first sign of victory was when I was able to recover my erring sight. When my voice awakened Li-Li from her sleep and she sat up, the satin curves of her body undulating languidly on the bed. Rapturously she turned her gaze on me. Desperately I fought, my whole being torn with anguish, just as she was torn with anguish – the anguish of joy and pure exhilaration. Then she got up and stood leaning out of the window. That instant I looked away and I returned to my senses – a ruin, the very dregs of a life.

I looked up to the sky in my gratitude. I was no longer myself. My stock of faith I lost in the raging battle. In triumph and with a bleeding heart I went down. Prayer is the balm. I turned my face to the *Kiblah* and prepared to pray.

They were still prostrate when the sun shone down on the nave. Some had gone to sleep, others were snoring, and the rest were lost in private meditation. They were all still waiting for the words 'God is greatest' when a sudden raucous laugh burst upon them. It was Me'eza the Dope who was in the habit of seeking refuge in the mosque whenever his wife turned him out of the house. He nearly split his sides laughing before his words came; sheer drivel, but at least they came.

'Look at the dopes,' he said, 'praying without a leader.'

In triumph and with a bleeding heart, I went down. Prayer is the balm. I turned my face to the *Kiblah* and prepared to pray. I opened my eyes and Li-Li's naked form appeared before me, throbbing, voluptuous, her silken hair falling in ripples down her sides. Forgive me oh God, for I have concealed from You the truth. The devil has won the day.

While all were kneeling together, like a stray flock come home, I stole through the window by the *Kiblah* and in a flash I was knocking at the door on the second floor of the house opposite. Wrapped in a bed-sheet Li-Li opened the door.

'I have come to teach you to pray,' I said with terror in my smile as I started to unbutton my cloak. The bed-sheet slipped from her shoulder. Sharply she pulled it back.

'Sorry, I bought the English record that teaches prayer. I found I understand it better,' she said as she turned her back and switched off the light.

Did you have to turn on the light, Li-Li?

Death from Old Age

It was on just such a morning that Am Mohamed died. What annoyed me was that people took his death as a matter of course, no reason for anyone to grieve or mourn or even to sigh in sorrow.

That day I had started work as usual signing birth certificates which made regular citizens, recognized by the state, out of new-born infants. As a matter of fact my job reminded me of Sayyedna Radwan, guardian of the here-after. For just as no one could leave or enter that abode without his sanction, no one could enter or depart from this world without mine.

I used to start the day warranting certificates with a long queue of mothers standing in front of me waiting to have their infants' vaccinations checked. Forty days ago these infants were only a name on a slip of paper, and now they already had a few weeks of life behind them and incipient problems. I rather enjoyed my work in spite of the many troubles I was bound to encounter. It was refreshing every morning to inspect the tiny mites so full of the vigour of new life. Their mothers were all young and newly married and happy to be mothers. They'd probably started to collect since early morning in their best clothes, their eye-brows freshly pencilled and their eyes carefully lined with kohl. It was no use trying to keep their line straight for they kept on falling out to go and look at some other woman to see what she was wearing and take a peep at her infant to compare it with their own. There was no malice intended, of course, but they all saw to it that their babies were properly decked with wolves' teeth and amulets, and the first thing they did when they got home was to read the charms against the evil eye.

After the women it was the schoolchildren's turn to line
up. Their noisy clatter filled the room. The same children
who not so long ago had been carried in here in their
mothers' arms. Now they were back again on their own
two feet to get certificates from the office to admit them to
school. Then there were the young workers; boys and girls
who came for a statement that they were above twelve
years of age, which the law on the employment of juveniles
required before they were allowed to embark on their
lifelong struggle for their daily bread. That lot was never
noisy. They just stood, dazed and bewildered, with the awed
look of those about to probe a dark interior.

By the time I was through with them I could tell from
the racket outside that the next batch was collecting. Male
voices in an uproar of oaths with angry references to justice
and humanity and the government and the waste of time.
Nothing would calm that lot. Not even the repeated assurances of the orderly who vainly tried to keep their line
straight, his fist tightly clasped on the measly tips he was
collecting from them. He shook his head many times and
assured them they would all take their turn. Yes, they
will be granted leave. Yes, they will pass the medical
examination. Dr Khaled is a kind man. Yes, he is in a good
mood today. Just a little patience friends, and you'll get
your ages estimated. You'll all be getting what you came
for. Everything in good time. Just a little patience. Then
they started trailing in, a long queue of people obviously
unused to discipline. All you saw was the restless faces of
men caught up in a mad race to grab the loaf out of the
other fellow's mouth. Coarse boorish faces bruised and
toughened by the daily encounter with life in the raw.

By ten o'clock I was through with the world of infants
and youngsters and adults and I prepared to enter the
sphere of the dead. They, too, have their problems. Death
is by no means the end of a man. As a matter of fact in
dying a man gives a lot more trouble than he ever did
while he lived. If the penalty for smuggling someone into

the world without a birth certificate is a fine of one pound, the penalty for smuggling him out without a licence is a term of imprisonment. And while the state never bothered much about an individual during his lifetime, it suddenly gives him the greatest attention the moment he expires. Just as the law cares nothing for how he lived but will move heaven and earth to know how he died.

Suspicion in some cases is a crime, goes the saying. But the legislator takes the opposite view : that it is a virtue in most cases. Accordingly, anyone who dies is assumed to have been murdered until it is proved otherwise. It was my job to get 'otherwise' proved. My job was to certify the death, to examine the body, and to sniff for evidence of foul play. And after having made an approximate guess as to the cause of death, put it down on the death certificate. Only then did the deceased have a right to get buried and start off for the next world.

At ten o'clock then, my dealings with the world of the dead began. The first people I had to see from that sphere were the undertakers' assistants when they came in and crowded round my desk. Am Mohamed used to be one of them. I never noticed him at the beginning for they all looked alike. And although assistants are usually associated with the young, those were a curious lot, the youngest of them well over sixty-five. There was something unwholesome in their senility, unlike the common run of pensioned or retired officials many of whom retained a youthful appearance in spite of their grey hair and wrinkles and rounded backs. These men were somehow disfigured by old age. Their bodies were shrunk to a feeble tottering frame, and their faces were shrivelled and dry as a raisin. The tall appeared taller, and the thin appeared thinner, while the short could hardly be seen. Invariably there was a white stubble sprouting on their thin haggard faces, and their eyes were bleary from more than one disease. Their work-clothes may have differed in colour and quality but they were all equally old and worn, and reached no lower than the knee. Their headgear, too, was the same for all. A long narrow rag of some sort, wound round a frayed, shapeless head-cover of some sort, or simply round their naked pates.

They were quite something to look at, what with their great age and the way they were rigged out, in addition to their many infirmities. They looked like creatures from a distant planet where everything is moth-eaten and decrepit.

Their work began from the moment a man gave up the ghost. Just like the angels who conveyed the soul to heaven, these undertakers' assistants took care of the departed until they got him safely underground. Some people imagine that the undertaker's job is easy, but in reality it is much more difficult than simply conveying the soul to heaven. Some may also be under the impression that it is an unpleasant job, which is another mistaken notion. It is a job like any other. If people work only to make a living then any job is unpleasant, which means that work must have rules and regulations. Here the rule was for the boss to sit in the shop and receive the death notices. It was he who dealt with the clients and cashed in advance payments, and only in rare cases did he personally undertake to wash the deceased.

After he clinched a deal, his assistants took over. They'd run to the house of the deceased in order to get him dressed. Then run for the doctor at the Health Department office. Then back to the shop or to the herbalist's. It was they who had to heat the water and carry the body on their lean arms to the wash-basin and wrap it in the shroud before they placed it in the coffin. Sometimes too they were made to help carry the coffin to the mosque or to the graveyard. The coffin usually had long rough handles of unpolished wood that settled viciously on the lean old neck, sometimes making it bleed. Very often it was heavy, and the distance always long. Summertime was hell. But the biggest torture were the obese.

So at ten o'clock it was their turn to come in, crowding before me, each of them stretching a skinny arm with a death notice. Each trying to get me to start off with him first, to see his client and give him the burial licence which would allow him to get on with his work before it got late.

There was something in those boys at once pathetic and grotesque. I couldn't resist a quip sometimes.

'And when shall we be writing out one for you too?' I used to say to the first of them to reach my desk.

The poor devil could only laugh. They were always anxious to please me, and they generally went along with anything I said. That's why I was astonished one day when one of them did not respond when I made the same quip to him. I stared at the man. He looked just like the others. The only difference I noticed was that a slight shadow covered both his eyes like a winter cloud.

'What's wrong with you?' I asked, seeing that something was obviously wrong.

'I wish I'd died in her place,' he moaned sadly.

'In whose place?'

'Didn't you hear? My daughter. She died.'

'When?'

'Yesterday. The primus stove blew up in her face. She died in the hospital.'

I didn't believe him, for his blank expression hardly altered as he announced this news. I had to ask his Mo'allem, who was not his boss alone but that of three others as well, all equally ancient. This one did not conform to the traditional image of mo'allems, who were usually corpulent hulks with fearsome moustaches. He was only in his thirties, tanned and clean-shaven with a severe expression on his face though at heart he loved to frolic. The business had come to him upon his father's death but not before he had sown his wild oats and knocked about for a while. Looking at him anyone could see he was sharp and clear-witted and knew what he was about. Although he was young he wore the traditional dress of well-to-do mo'allems : a bright red tarboosh and a woollen cloak over his silk caftan, the rich embroidery round the neckline showing through the opening in the cloak. He wore elegant black shoes and in his hand he held the inevitable amber beads.

He confirmed what the man said. It was true that his
daughter had died in hospital and that by her death he
was left alone in the world. I felt sorry for him as he stood
so forlorn, leaning towards the ground as if an invisible
force were pulling him down, precipitating the moment
when he would be laid there for good. He just stood,
motionless and dry-eyed.

'Ah well, Am Mohamed,' I said, 'don't upset yourself.
This is the way of the world.'

As I said that, I realized I was not even sure of the man's
name, I was only guessing it was Mohamed. Actually I
called them all Mohamed and out of deference to me they
all answered to that, as if it didn't matter to them any more
whether they had a name of their own.

'Yes,' he mumbled, 'I wish I'd died in her place.'

It is not uncommon to hear such expressions in circumstances of overwhelming grief and one takes them for what
they are, a mere burst of emotion. But in the case of Am
Mohamed the way he spoke left no doubt he meant what
he was saying.

From then on I began to take an interest in the man, as
well as in all the other Am Mohameds. I found out the
reason why they were all so old, almost as if to do their
job it was an essential requirement to be elderly. Most of
them, I discovered, were retired school janitors, office boys,
or police constables. They took odd jobs during the first
few years of their retirement until their strength was gone
and they were quite worn out. After that the only way for
them to make a living was as undertakers' assistants. That
is if they were lucky enough to find a vacancy. The job did
not require much physical strength, and the wages were
so poor that none would accept them – none but an old
man on the brink of death from weakness and starvation.
And yet, in spite of their years when the most they could do
was lie in their beds and wait for death to come, their duties
were most strenuous.

I'd gone with Mohamed on hundreds of calls, and every
time we went through the same act. He was always in a

hurry to get the burial licence from me in order to get on with his work in time to be able to attend to other business. There was the boss to consider, and like all apprentices he was anxious to please him. So he was always trying to dissuade me from going all the way to the house of the deceased as the journey back and forth took too long. He wanted me to sign without leaving my office. But orders were orders and mine were to examine the body before giving a licence. He used to get excited and swear to me that the death was natural, that there was not the slightest suspicion of foul play, that he himself had undressed the body and examined it. He had pulled the hair and stared into the eyes and felt the bones. My comfort was all he was interested in, he assured me every time. I'd shake my head stubbornly and he'd shake his in despair as he started to run in front of me. 'As you wish then,' he would say. 'Have it your way.'

After a while he would stop.

'I swear by God, my Bey, it's an old man this time. A simple case of death from old age.'

'Death from old age – in full possession of faculties,' was the term used in the case of an old person's death when no other cause of death is apparent. The phrase 'in full possession of faculties' is thrown in for legal purposes where a legacy is involved and litigations amongst heirs are likely to arise. It was a common expression widely used by health inspectors, civil servants and undertakers, and it was only natural for Am Mohamed to adopt it too.

Seeing that it was no use persuading me to stay back he would trot on in front of me to show me the way. We went to crowded areas; crowded with people and houses and flies and everything imaginable. There were more people than houses, and more houses than space, and about a million flies to each individual. Everything was piled up in heaps as if the work of someone in a hurry. And Am Mohamed trotted along on his skinny bow-legs, with sweat streaking his face, tinier in stature than a wizened monkey. It was a struggle for him to catch up with me and a struggle to run ahead of me, and a struggle to clear a path for me to proceed. Acting as self-appointed policeman he starts to direct the traffic, signalling carts to halt, and ordering vegetable hawkers to stop yelling and waving their arms about, and to make way for the 'Bey'. He gets out of breath but he manages to keep up some sort of dialogue with me to keep me entertained. He curses the crowds and those who disobey his orders. There's no good left in the world any more. In the old days death came in plenty, and business was good. I ask, panting like him, whether we still have far to go. Oh no, only a few steps, just round the corner. So I proceed and after hundreds of steps we have still not reached the house or the body. We keep winding in and out of lanes and alleys and the people who see us go by turn their faces away with a visible shudder, wondering whom we are after. Am Mohamed keeps trotting on, in front and behind and on both sides of me, trying his best to ward off the disaster of my losing patience and deciding to put off the business to the next day.

Finally we reach our destination. Am Mohamed picks up the hem of his *gallabieh* and holds it between his teeth as he rushes on double-quick to make way for me. No sooner do I step into the house than I am greeted with terrifying screams followed by a chorus of wails.

'The doctor has come for you, my love!' they cry, as if the doctor were Azrael himself. But Am Mohamed pays no attention.

'Hey, out of the way, you,' he shouts. 'This way, my Bey. Get out of the way, I said. God damn those women, where the hell do they all come from! This way, my Bey.'

The black bundles crowding the room begin to move but not before they have peered into my face to take a close look at the doctor. At last there is no one in the dead man's room but the nearest relative, Am Mohamed and myself.

'There, my Bey,' says Am Mohamed, rushing towards the body, hardly waiting to recover his breath. He rips the cover away to reveal the dead man.

'See? I told you, just dandy. Not a scratch.' He goes on as if in self-defence, wanting to prove he was right when he said the death was natural.

'Here's the chest. Look. And the belly. And here's the mouth, clean as a whistle. And the hair.' He pulls at the hair to show me there is no evidence of poison. He becomes irritable as it is nearly midday, and he wants to have finished by then.

'And the legs, here.' He pulls up the leg. 'I told you, my Bey, it is only old age. Look at the back.'

He tries to haul the body over but it proves beyond him even though he calls God's saints to his aid.

'Lay off, damn you,' his boss would scold gruffly as he takes over. But Mohamed insists on helping if only by supporting a leg, or straightening a finger.

When the examination was over and we have left the room, Am Mohamed would still not take his eyes off me, like a schoolboy awaiting the results of an examination. He breathed with relief only when I signed the certificate and he held it thankfully in his hand like a gift from heaven. Then he would bite on his gums and his pupils would dilate, and his smile would say, 'I told you so.' And he would scurry down ahead of me, back to my office.

One day I saw a tear in Am Mohamed's eye. A tiny liquid speck, as if it were the last drop in his sockets. It came after he'd received a quick slap on his face from the boss. He had made a mistake. I had gone to examine a body and it was still not undressed when I got there. Before I had time to reprove the boss for it, the latter had come down with a slap on Am Mohamed's face as if to show me it was not his mistake and that he had seen to it that justice was done. It made me furious but Am Mohamed never moved. He just stood with his hand on his cheek, a guilty expression on his face, like a reproved child.

One day I went to my office and found it packed with Am Mohameds, all standing glum and silent as usual, decrepitude having sapped them of even the energy to talk. I was not a little astonished when I found them crowd-

ing my office, for I was not used to having so many at a
time. As soon as he saw me their boss came forward with
a broad grin on his face wishing me every kind of good
morning, fragrant with jasmin and roses and honey dew,
which he accompanied by a great roar of laughter. Then,
as if he suddenly remembered something, his expression
changed. He stood with his fists resting on his belly and an
expression of profound grief on his face.

'Didn't you hear?'

'Hear what?'

'The man, he died.'

'What man?' I spoke carelessly as the boss was in the
habit of talking to me of people and things I had never
heard of as if I knew all about them.

'One of my boys.'

'You mean Mohamed?'

'That's right, God give you a long life.' Then immediately
his professional look came back and he was brisk and
businesslike. 'If you please doctor, for the sake of the
Prophet, kindly let us have the death certificate without
delay. You know, it's summer, and him an old man and all
that.'

I couldn't help a smile. Only yesterday Mohamed was
trotting all over me on our way to a call, and today he was
dead and his boss was as eager to rush him through his
own burial as he himself used to be for his clients.

'Well, my Bey, what do you say?'

'So he went and did it,' I murmured, addressing no one
in particular.

'That's right, and if God hadn't sent us a new boy,
heaven knows how we were going to manage today.'

'A new boy?'

'That's right. There he is. Come, Guindi.'

Guindi came. Another shrivelled old man no less decrepit
than the others. He hadn't got into his official clothes yet
for he was still wearing a crumpled, shapeless tarboosh.

'If you will be pleased to sign, my Bey,' the Mo'allem
was saying.

'No, I've got to see him first.'

'Well, it's not as if he's a stranger to you. I just don't want to put you to any trouble, that's all. I wouldn't be deceiving you; after all, he was an old man, and you knew him. You can sign right here, "old age", that's all there is to it.'

Here all his boys joined in to back him, eager to do their departed colleague a last good turn. But I insisted on what I said, if only to have one last look at Mohamed. After all, we were pals.

Presently, we left my office and set out for Am Mohamed's house. It was a grim procession, with me in the front and the Mo'allem at my side holding his *gallabieh* up by the hem with one hand while he gesticulated with the other, telling me all about Am Mohamed's funeral and how he was giving it to him free although times were bad, and one never knew. Behind us came the rest of the Mo'allem's crew. People stopped to stare as we went by, wondering who the eminent person could be whose death formalities required the whole lot of us.

The house where Am Mohamed lived was out of the way, at the foot of a hill. It consisted of a large courtyard with an enormous heap of garbage in the centre, surrounded by rooms, most of them dilapidated but not unoccupied in spite of that. Our arrival did not stir the slightest motion. Not a wail, not a cry, not a sob went up. Everything seemed to be going on much as usual, as if death had never called there. Only a few dogs began to bark when they saw us coming but they stopped and scampered away when the Mo'allem shouted at them.

The room was dark and only the open door let in some light. Am Mohamed was lying near the wall covered by old German newspapers; nobody could explain how they found their way there.

'Alright,' shouted the Mo'allem to the new boy.

The 'boy' bent down and removed the newspapers with trembling hands. Am Mohamed lay stretched out with his face to the wall like a punished child. He was wearing his work clothes, his body was shrunken, and his feet, so often seen scurrying as he went on his rounds, were now lying still in a thick cast of dried mud and dirt.

'There,' the Mo'allem was saying, 'nothing wrong at all. Turn him over, let the Bey see him properly.'

The old 'boy' tried to haul him over but the effort proved beyond him. I could imagine then old Am Mohamed rising from the dead and reproving him in his own gruff way.

'Lay off, damn you. Here, my Bey, I'll turn myself over. No need for you to trouble. Here I am, absolutely nothing wrong. Here are my legs.' And he stretched out his legs, two long desiccated twigs. He took off his clothes and stood naked in the middle of the room, a skeleton in a covering of skin with not an ounce of flesh between. Am Mohamed turned himself round. 'I told you, my Bey, I'm an old man. Here's my arm.'

He tried to stretch his arm but it seems the rheumatism which had long troubled him when he was alive had left him with stiff joints so he gave up and went on to show his head, a little shrunken ball, the cheeks sucked into the mouth, and one jaw clamped on the other.

'And here's my hair,' he said, pulling at the little that was left, 'and my feet,' he added sticking out his two colourless feet that looked as if they had been dead for decades.

The effort of thus displaying himself must have tired him for he lay down again turning his face to the wall.

'You could have spared yourself the trouble. I told you, it's only "old age",' and he sighed as he settled down.

I came round to myself at the sound of the Mo'allem's voice.

'Well?' he was saying.

'You may go ahead.'

Immediately a great bustle started as the Mo'allem removed his cloak and stood like a captain on deck briskly giving out orders.

After a while Am Mohamed was settled in his coffin and the coffin was settled on the bearers' backs, all of them his pals. They started on their way, the coffin swaying as they carried it out of the house where not a sound or a single wail went up to bid farewell to Am Mohamed.

After the Mo'allem had checked that everything was all over and that he had done his duty in giving his 'boy' a decent funeral, I was surprised to see him suddenly go back and squat on the ground near the wall, hiding his head between his knees. I saw him give vent to a long muffled sob, and in a low sad lament he called Am Mohamed's name over and over.

When his sobs subsided, remembering formalities, he lifted a tear-stained face to me.

'You did sign the licence, Doctor, didn't you?'

I nodded.

'Wasn't it . . .'

'Yes, "old age".'

He wiped the tears from his eyes.

'And "in full possession of faculties" . . .'

'That's right. "In full possession of faculties",' I replied.

Bringing in the Bride

The fact that the people of El Sharkieh province, where I come from, are generous goes without saying. But their being so impetuous in their generosity as to 'bring in the bride' is another matter. In fact it was a strange custom of theirs which they stopped only about two years ago.

When a country girl married into another town it was usual, on the wedding day, for her entire family to go with her to the groom's town. And since the roads in those far-flung provinces were not safe in those days, it was also the custom for the family to be accompanied by a great number of the people of the town, walking in a long procession headed by the camel on which the bride rode, and which was usually led by the groom himself or a man who was his deputy.

That was not unusual, indeed it was the custom in all country weddings all over Egypt. But what was unusual, and unique to the province of El Sharkieh, was that when the bride and her procession passed by the towns and farms lying on the way, the people from those places, young and old, would all come out to greet them and invite them to call on their respective homesteads. And to prove the sincerity of the invitation they'd have a beast slaughtered and its head impaled on a long pole. They would wait until the procession drew near and then go forward to meet them, presenting them with a *fait accompli* by saying, 'Kindly step this way. The beast is slaughtered and your dinner is prepared. Tonight you will be our guests.'

Naturally the bride's people could not accept the invitation, explaining that this was the wedding night and that there was no time to pay calls or accept hospitality on the way. The hosts would not accept the excuse, taking the refusal as an insult, whereupon they would insist more vehemently while the bride's people refused more emphatically. Very often the contest ended with a brawl involving violence and abuse and not infrequently a few dead or wounded. But invariably it ended in one of two ways : either the bride's party won and proceeded unmolested to their destination, or the other party won, in which case the defeated company was led forcibly into the town and compelled to accept the hospitality. In most cases it was the bride's people who triumphed because it was their pride and honour they were defending. Whereas in the case of the people of the various towns it was merely a perfunctory show they put up to demonstrate their generosity but not to the extent of exposing themselves to danger.

This had been the custom for centuries until at last it was abolished, but only in recent times. The reason was a young girl from the village of Kafr Azab who was betrothed to a man from another town. On the day of the wedding the whole town went out as usual to see her to her new dwelling. On the way they were stopped by a huge black giant who stood in the middle of the road barring their way. No sooner had the people laid eyes on him than they were seized by panic since they were not particularly noted for their courage. Originally, Kafr Azab had consisted of a number of big families who had gradually disintegrated because of poverty and the scarcity of land. Eventually it deteriorated into a hamlet inhabited by thousands of belligerent individuals callously bent on destroying one another. They were all petty landowners, who owned at most only a fraction of a *feddan* and whose greatest ambition was to bring that fraction up to a whole. Their merchants – if they could be called that – were mere hawkers who carried their wares in bundles which they hauled on their shoulders on market-days. There were at least fifty grocery shops in the village, none of whose capital exceeded fifty pounds. There were hundreds whose only profession was to make tea and coffee and whose only capital was the tea kettle and the tumbledown shack where they lodged. There were men of religion and Koran chanters and *ta'amiyeh*[1] vendors who stood selling, after prayers, at the door of the mosque. There were basket-weavers and story-tellers and petty thieves and brigands in abundance. If there was a vacancy for a watchman's job there would be a hundred applicants, all falling over one another to get it. A man who managed to find employment superintending cotton-worm pickers during the picking season considered himself born under a lucky star.

Yet in spite of their dire poverty, or perhaps because of it, they never ceased from lodging complaints against one another. Reports from Kafr Azab of attempted murder, armed robbery or rape never stopped pouring into the police station. The smart ones were those who filled their pockets without worrying how. A man who skimped and pinched to save one millieme was a man with talent. A land superintendent who set a price on his signature was considered smart. But the cleverest of all was the Omdah who reached his post by trading in cotton, nominally from the second crop, but actually stolen from the fields. So it was not surprising for anyone from Kafr Azab, when such things as honour and courage were spoken of, to turn down his lip and ask with contempt, 'How much is that worth on the market?'

That day they dutifully set out behind the bride to see her to her new home. Their real motive was the sumptuous wedding dinner they were hoping to get on the way. Potatoes and heaps of meat covered with hot, freshly baked bread, not to mention the sweet courses and the free entertainment, perhaps even a cigarette to crown the day.

It is not hard to imagine their apprehension then, on seeing that black giant rising against the skyline to bar their way. Panic-stricken, their ranks broke up and they whispered amongst themselves and craned their necks to see what was up. They had no one they could delegate to

[1] Bean rissoles.

negotiate with the giant as they had no leader. As a matter
of fact the people of Kafr Azab had never been too keen on
appointing a leader as each one of them wanted that role
for himself. But in this instance leadership was fraught
with danger and it took them a long time to find someone
willing to speak on their behalf.

Some suggested Sheikh Ragab Abou Shama'a. Not
because he was the owner of three whole *feddans* which he
had bought inch by inch through depriving himself and his
children of his own buffalo's milk, but because he was the
wisest and most moderate. In other words the most timor-
ous. It was wise to have such a man for a leader in a
situation where daring could be foolish, perhaps even bor-
dering on ill-manners.

Sheikh Ragab accepted with great reluctance and only
after he had been begged several times. He shouted at the
procession to be silent. Then he kicked his stumpy little
donkey and trotted up to the giant, dismounting respectfully within a little distance.

'Good day to you,' he said in the fawning tone which
distinguished the inhabitants of Kafr Azab.

'Good day nothing,' returned the giant peremptorily, his
eyes letting off sparks, 'you turn right this way.'

'Where to, if you please?' asked Sheikh Ragab even
more unctuously, feigning total innocence.

'You're our guests for the night.'

'Whose guests, pray?'

'You're the guests of El Sandik Bey. We're his men, and
I'm Ambar, his servant.'

Sheikh Ragab tried every means by which to extricate
himself from the situation. He even enquired after the
impaled head of the slaughtered animal, pleading that since
it wasn't there they had a right to decline the invitation.
But he was told in a manner which couldn't stand argument
that the beast had actually been slaughtered and that they
had no choice but to comply by good means or bad. A few
of the younger men did not seem to appreciate Ambar's
peremptory attitude so they raised a protest of some sort,

aiming at least to impress the womenfolk. They even raised
their sticks in preparation for battle, but Sheikh Ragab
waved a commanding hand and shouted at them to be
silent. He was too well acquainted with their calibre. He
also knew in advance the outcome of any fight in which they
engaged. For no sooner would the fight have started than
they would take to their heels, having dealt a perfunctory
blow or two, just for the record.

'Well, just what is it you want, friend?' asked Sheikh
Ragab.

'We want you to call on our farm without another word,'
replied Ambar.

'By all means,' said Sheikh Ragab, kicking his donkey
again, 'we shall be honoured to be your guests, just don't
upset yourself. This way boys!' he shouted at his company
as he motioned for them to follow him.

The enormous Ambar couldn't help raising an eyebrow
at this sudden and unexpected capitulation which robbed
him of the fight he was looking forward to bragging about
for days to come. He marvelled at these people who laid
no store by their pride. Nevertheless he took the camel by the
bridle and led the way to the farm, followed by no less than
five hundred of the inhabitants of Kafr Azab, some riding,
some walking with their slippers tucked under their arms
and the hems of their *gallabiehs* caught between their teeth.
Some were walking behind their mounts, following their
well-known maxim : Better to degrade yourself than your
mount.

Shortly they came within sight of the El Sandik farm.
Attracted by the noise, the Bey came out to watch what he
thought was a fellaheen wedding procession, but he was
astounded to see the crowd stop at his gate, led by no less
than Ambar, his servant.

'Wait here and don't move,' said Ambar to Sheikh Ragab.

He left them there and turned towards his master with
much the same demeanour as Tarek Ibn Ziad after he had
conquered Spain.

'My Bey, we've brought in the bride,' he announced in

the tone of a victorious hero.

The Bey only stared at him, unable to understand. Suddenly he seemed to remember having heard of some such custom. His father had told him. But then that was a long time ago when he was only a boy, in his father's day and his grandfather's before him. Those were the days of plenty when he heard it said they had owned one thousand five hundred *feddans* and four thousand head of sheep. But where was all this now? The land was gone and so were the days of plenty. The guest house was torn down, and the crop was mortgaged to several banks even before it was harvested. Only Ambar remained from those better days. The last of the family slaves from the days when they used to own them by the score. And now the fool goes and asks in those cohorts from Kafr Azab. A famished, worn-out battalion who must have starved themselves for days in preparation for the wedding feast.

Blows and torrents of abuse fell on the miserable and uncomprehending Ambar. What had he done wrong? How many times in the past, in the days of the Bey's father, had he brought in brides to call at their farm only to be commended and praised, and generously rewarded? And now he gets beaten for his good work. Surely, it seems, masters too have gone bad like the times. Gone are the days of lordly hospitality when the Bey would have taken pride in the bride's acceptance of his invitation instead of flying into such a rage.

The Bey gave his servant one of two choices : either he get rid of that crowd or he would shoot him dead. Ambar understandably opted for the first and he was back like a shot to negotiate with Sheikh Ragab. The fiery sparks were gone from his eyes, his features drooped sadly. It was his turn now to speak unctuously, apologizing profusely, explaining it was all a misunderstanding, that the Bey knew nothing of all this, taking all the blame on himself.

But there was nothing doing with Sheikh Ragab, who sat up in the saddle and declared to Ambar, backed by all five hundred of the inhabitants of Kafr Azab, that they were

there to stay. Their dignity would not let them turn back,
having come this far on the persistent invitation of El
Sandik Bey who was bound to honour his word. This was
perhaps the first time in their history that the people of
Kafr Azab had ever stuck together.

The footsore Ambar kept shuttling backwards and
forwards from the Bey to Sheikh Ragab, conveying messages, taking care to conceal what the one said of the other
and hoping all the time that his efforts would succeed. All
in vain.

When it became clear to the Bey that if he persisted in
withdrawing his invitation he was going to be exposed to all
and sundry as a miserable miser and made the laughing
stock of the area for miles around there was nothing for him
but to take them in. All night he was on his feet arranging
for covers and plates and food to fill up those hundreds of
hungry stomachs. But the first thing he did in the morning
was to sack Ambar, preferring to part with that last vestige
of grandeur rather than suffer any future disasters the latter
might bring on him.

As for the bride's company, having contentedly sipped
their morning coffee, and drawn on their first cigarettes,
they started on the remainder of their journey with no end
of praise for Sheikh Ragab and his wisdom. Any doubts as
to Sheikh Ragab's ability as a leader were completely dispelled and from now on they all became his staunch
followers. They even went so far as to hold the bride's
camel back, making way for Sheikh Ragab to ride at the
head of their procession.

No sooner had they left the El Sandik farm behind, their
hearty laughter rising from their satiated bellies, than they
were stopped by a crowd representing the people of El
Roda who had been waiting for them by the bridge. They
went through the same motions, Sheikh Ragab affecting
the same innocence. Hardly had the word 'invitation'
slipped from their leader than Sheikh Ragab was already
heading for their village, waving for the rest to follow.

Thus the village of El Roda found itself in a predicament, for how could they accommodate five hundred people when its own population did not exceed two hundred? In vain they struggled to extricate themselves, arguing that they were not adequately prepared. But Sheikh Ragab made further argument impossible by declaring blandly that 'anything will do'.

And so they progressed from town to town, and from village to village, even if they were stopped by only one man, and no matter how obviously perfunctory the invitation appeared. They reached their destination after seven days, eating, drinking and smoking, free. Even their mounts had fed lavishly on barley and clover and beans.

After this, the people of El Sharkieh province decided it would be wiser after all to curb their generosity, and eventually they renounced the custom of bringing in brides.

The Shame

I believe they still refer to love as The Shame over there. They probably still hesitate to talk about it openly, making only covert allusions, even though you can see it in the hazy look in their eyes, and when the girls blush and shyly look down.

Like any other, the farm was not a big one. The few houses were built with their backs to the outside, the doors opening onto an inner courtyard where they celebrated their weddings and hung their calves when a sick one was slaughtered to be sold by the *oke*[1] or in lots. Events were few and could be foretold in advance. Day began before sunrise and ended after sunset. The favourite place was in the doorway where a north breeze blew and where it was pleasant to doze at noon and play a game of *siga*.[2]

Nothing much happened, and whatever did happen was predictable. You could be sure for instance that the scrawny little girl playing hopscotch would marry in a few years. Her complexion would clear and her angular body would take on softer curves, and she'd end up with one of those boys in tattered *gallabiehs* next to their skin, diving off the bridge like chained monkeys to swim in the canal.

Sometimes things did happen that were neither expected nor predictable. Like the day screams were heard coming from the field. They ripped the vast emptiness of the countryside, warning of some fearsome event. And although at first the people did not know where the sound was coming from they found themselves running to help, or at

[1] One *oke* is equivalent to approximately 1¼ kilograms.
[2] A game of draughts where pebbles are used for pieces and the ground serves for a board.

least to find out what had happened. But that day there
was no need for help. The men returning to the farm tried
to avoid answering when the women asked what had
happened. For they could not bring themselves to say that
Fatma had been caught in the maize field with Gharib.
For both were no strangers to the farm. Fatma was Farag's
sister, and Gharib was Abdoun's son and the matter had
been plain to all.

It was a small farm where everybody knew everybody
else, and private affairs did not remain private. People
even knew when someone had money hoarded away,
exactly how much, where it was kept, and how it could be
stolen if one had a mind to. Except that no one ever stole
from another. If at all, they stole from the farm crops;
petty thefts like a lapful of cotton or some corn-cobs. Or
sometimes they would dip into the drainage canal of a
rice field when the watchman wasn't looking, and take all
the fish without sharing it with the bailiff as the understanding went.

Everyone knew Fatma and all there was to know about
her. Not that she had a reputation or anything like that.
It was just that she was pretty; or to be more accurate the
prettiest girl on the farm. But that was not the point, for
if a fair skin was the yardstick by which beauty is measured
in the countryside, Fatma was dark. The point was that no
one could explain what it was about that girl that made
her so different from the others. Her cheeks were hale and
ruddy giving the impression that she had honey for breakfast and chicken and pigeon for lunch, when her daily
fare was plain curd cheese and pickled peppers, onions
and scorched fry. Her eyes were black and beady and
incessantly alive with a piercing look which made it hard
to hold them for long. To say that her hair was soft and
black, and that her floating black gown did not conceal
her provoking curves would not do her justice. It was not
her looks that made her what she was, but her intense
femininity. A gushing, throbbing, devastating force which
it was hard to trace to any definite source. The way she

smiled, the way she turned her head to look behind her,
the way she asked someone to help her with her water jar;
her every movement was a provocation. There was witchery
in the way she tied her only cabbage-green headcloth at a
slant to reveal her smooth black hair. There was witchery
in the dimples in her cheeks when she smiled, and in the
trail of her rippling laughter; in the very sound of her
languid, fluid voice which she knew how to modulate and
distil into drops of the purest female seduction, every single
drop of which could quench the lust of a dozen males.

Fatma aroused men, almost as if she was made for that.
She even aroused the dormant virility in little boys. When
they saw her coming, they felt a sudden urge to uncover
themselves. And they often did, raising their *gallabiehs*
well up above their knees, and no amount of shouting or
scolding would make them let up, for they themselves could
not explain this urge to expose themselves in her presence.

That's why she was a worry to Farag, her brother, who
was a poor lonesome fellah who owned nothing but his
cow. The bailiff would not let him have more than three
feddans to cultivate. His attempts every year to increase
his share by half a *feddan* invariably ended in failure.
Nevertheless he was a strapping hulk of a man. In one meal
he could devour three whole loaves of bread, if he had
them, and down the entire contents of the water cooler in
one gulp. The calf of his leg had the proportions of a thigh.
But his life was a torment on account of his sister. She
lived with him and his wife who had a flat nose and a pale
face and was a good sort on the whole, except when she
drew Farag's attention to his sister's breasts, insisting that
Fatma wobbled them on purpose when she walked. Also to
the kohl with which she lavishly bespattered her eyes, and
the chewing gum she was always asking people going to
market to bring her. Farag had no need to be reminded of
all this. He could see for himself, and it made his blood
boil. Yet he had no real reason to reprove Fatma. She was
no different from the other girls. They all dressed alike,
they all smeared their eyes with kohl, and they all chewed

gum. She was never caught in dubious situations, and her conduct was above reproach. Even when his wife accused her of colouring her cheeks with the wrapping paper of tobacco cartons, he had unwound his turban and wetted one corner with his spittle and rubbed her cheeks with it until he nearly drew blood, but nothing had come out. All he could do that day was glower at her, contenting himself with giving her a sharp scolding, while Fatma could think of no reason why she deserved to be treated that way. Warned and threatened by Farag, she well understood the meaning of The Shame. She was not guilty of it, nor did it even cross her mind to contemplate it. Indeed she would rather have died.

Because she knew that people loved and spoiled her, she behaved like anyone used to receiving affection. She was natural, and her reactions came from her heart. She knew her looks were what attracted people to her so she took care of them, never appearing unwashed or uncombed. When she worked on the fields she protected her hands from getting scratched by slipping on the socks she borrowed from Om[3] George. She was even careful not to offend when she spoke by using bad language or coarse expressions. Everyone loved her; everyone was her friend, and she loved them all in return. That was why she could not understand why her brother was so harsh with her, or the reason for the poisonous looks he kept darting at her.

Nor did Farag himself. All he knew was that he had to answer for his sister and for her screaming femininity. Every lustful look directed at her dug into his flesh. He could not wait to marry her off, preferably in another town, and rid himself of the responsibility. But in this respect Fatma was not doing so well; suitors were few, or none to speak of. For who was the fool who would want to be saddled with that heap of seduction? And once married what was he

[3] A respectful form of address to married women in rural society, the name being derived from the name of the person's son. This Coptic woman has a son called George, therefore she is addressed as Om George: mother of George.

going to do with her? People in those parts did not marry
in order to enjoy beauty and then put up walls to protect
it, because in the first place they did not live for enjoy-
ment. They were happy enough to survive. When they
married it was for the sake of an extra pair of hands, and
eventually a progeny to swell the labour force. For this
reason Fatma remained without suitors.

Not that the farm lacked men or young boys, and Fatma
like other girls worked as hard as any of them, going to the
fields at dawn and returning with the call for prayer at
sunset. But unlike the other girls she stirred trouble wherever she went. That's why Farag lived in constant fear
which he concealed behind a boisterous front. Much of
the jolly atmosphere of the farm came from him when he
fooled around with the men and made a mockery of their
false airs of decorum. He challenged the boys to swimming
races, and toppled baskets off the women's heads, and even
the most demure did not escape his pranks. At weddings
he wore his white *gallabieh* and his raw silk turban and
cropped his hair short; he shaved his beard smooth and
danced for the groom. He never failed to shower the bride
with the traditional gift of money, not forgetting the bailiff
and the cattle overseer, and anyone else standing around.
All from the money he made on the side stealing cotton
from the storehouse, or filching a bale on its way to the
truck.

He spent lavishly and filled the farm with his exuberance,
and he was popular everywhere. So that though his sister's
irresistible appeal caused even the stones to stir, and though
the men, torn with their passion, smouldered with desire
for her, Farag was a friend to them all. In deference to him
they looked away when they met Fatma, and when one of
them allowed a sigh to escape, someone was always there
to call him to order.

And so Fatma remained like a luscious fruit, ripe yet
forbidden. None came near her, or allowed anyone else to
come near her, while their hearts continued to pine. Old
and young lusted for her. But Farag was always there. His

wild laughter reminded them of his presence and warned them of The Shame, and they would return to their senses and rush to perform their afternoon prayers, or go round to the corner shop for a glass of tea.

And today she was caught in the maize field.

Not for the first time. She was always being caught with someone. Now in the maize field, now behind the stables, now under the thresher. Always by imagination. Rumours which invariably turned out to be false. For there was bound to be rumour wherever she went, just as sighs were bound to rise in her wake.

There was no malice in the people. They were decent kindly folk who wished for others what they wished for themselves. You could see their goodness even in their geese as they collected near the threshing floor, and cackled down to the canal to splash about and teach their young to swim. At sunset they returned, hundreds of them cackling back to their pens which they found by instinct. And when a foolish one strayed into a neighbour's pen by mistake, your neighbour would be at your door with the stray creature even before you realized it was missing.

Everyone on the farm was under Fatma's spell. She was loved by all. If she went to a wedding it was she who outshone the bride. This strange magnetism was the reason why they feared for her. They feared she might slip, for they could not believe a woman so desirable could long resist The Shame. Their conviction of this even led them to pick the man with whom she was likely to commit The Shame, and that was Gharib.

Gharib was the son of Abdoun. In spite of his age no one called Abdoun 'uncle'. He was an irritable old man addicted to chewing tobacco and drinking sugarless coffee. He quarrelled on the slightest provocation. Even the bailiff took care to keep out of his way. He was never known to have had a decent word for anyone. His talent for swearing was revealed at its best when a calamity befell the farm. Then he would take his position by the canal, like a bird of ill omen, and holding his *gallabieh* up by the hem, he

would curse and swear, at the same time spewing out his
tobacco chew and spluttering abuse on the peasants as if
they alone were responsible for the misfortune. But nobody
seemed to mind him for they knew there was no harm in
him.

As for Gharib, he was mistrusted by all. He was rude
and impudent, and he grew a forelock which he was fond
of showing off, smooth and shining beneath his white
woollen skull-cap. What's more, he had an eye for women
and thought nothing of setting out to seduce them – which
was why people were wary of him – without much caring
whose wife it happened to be.

In spite of his father's ungainly appearance, Gharib was
a good-looking boy, and although weather-beaten, his
complexion was not too dark. He spoke little but his speech
was engaging, perhaps because he sounded so carefree,
speaking with the raucous rasp of an adolescent. Somehow
he escaped the doltish look common to peasant boys, his
clothes were always clean, and he was quick and sharp-
witted which was probably what made him so smug. He
worked tirelessly, and sang lays, and he owned his own
equipment for making tea which he was always pressing on
his friends. When night fell, he could not bear the narrow
confines of his house, and he would go outside to seek the
comfort of the hay near the barn. There he would sit,
proudly feeling his thighs and his chest, and brag to his
friends about his amorous exploits – a field where he was
highly proficient and they were hopelessly inept.

His flirting was flagrant and undisguised. He would eye
the women boldly from the legs up, with a glint of irony
in his look, or it could have been a repressed chuckle. He
couldn't help it if his look unsettled them. A woman knew
when he looked at her that way that he divined her
thoughts, and if her thoughts were dwelling on The Shame,
which more often than not was the case, she would realize
he was stripping her with his eyes and she would get so
confused trying to cover herself up that her defences would
weaken and she could not help but succumb. As the number

of his victims grew, so did his vanity, and the glint in his eye became bolder still.

There was something in the boy that set him apart from other men. Perhaps it was his intense virility. It was enough for a woman to catch sight of the back of his neck or the cord of his underpants for her limbs to melt. He didn't worry much about his methods. All means were fair which led him to a woman. At weddings he used to force himself into their midst making them freeze where they stood. At the mill he was only too pleased to carry their baskets or turn the wheel of their hoppers. Even the sick he did not spare. And except for his fear of the bailiff's rifle he might even have sneaked in to Om George by night. When people complained to Abdoun, he flared up at them, his face contorted into an angry scowl. 'There he is,' he would say, 'do what you like with him. I wash my hands.'

But there was nothing much anyone could do. For though Gharib was short he had the strength of a bullock. He was quite capable of lifting the heavy iron water-wheel with one hand while he broke a man's neck with the other, the same ironical glint never leaving his eye.

Of all the men he was the most virile, and of all the women Fatma was the most seductive, and it was only natural that they should be coupled by gossip. And yet they were poles apart. Fatma avoided him because of his reputation, while secretly he was intimidated by her. Although he could deftly handle the bailiff's servant girl, or Shafia, the widow with the many children, when it came to Fatma it was a different matter. For Fatma was a creature apart.

Sometimes he liked to brag to the boys, sleeping on the hay with him, that she was in love with him, and that she sent him messages. But he was the first one to despise himself for his vain boasts. He worked in the fields like a stallion, everywhere sweeping the women off their feet with his irresistible appeal. But with Fatma he was quite powerless. For her part she feared him, so that if he happened to greet her, his heart pounding as he did so, her reply would come curt and timid. She feared him because she feared The Shame while he feared her because he feared to fail, and all the time their names continued to be linked and Farag continued to hide his misgivings behind his show of goodwill, while playing up to Gharib who was the source of his greatest fears. It all went on covertly. On the face of it they were all happy kinsfolk living in brotherhood, and the farm was small and Abdoun's house was only three houses away to the right of Farag's, and there were practically no incidents of geese going astray.

Meanwhile they all lived on the brink of expectation. Things were bound to come to a head, like waking up in the middle of the night at the sound of a gun-shot or a cry coming from the fields to announce she had been caught there with Gharib.

It wasn't long before it happened.

It took no one by surprise. They took the incident for granted as something they had expected sooner or later. Even the children – in their private world where they fabricate their own gossip and hold their own notions about grown-ups – even they realized that Fatma at last had committed the forbidden thing their parents had long warned them against. Fatma had committed The Shame.

So when they saw Farag leaving the field for the first time without his turban, his head uncovered, his waistcoat unbuttoned, with mud clinging to his trousers, and when they saw his ashen face and trembling moustache, and his bloodshot eyes, they huddled close to the stable wall as, instinctively, they felt the enormity of what had befallen Farag. They followed him stealthily through the gateway of the farm until he reached his house. They saw him bawl at his young son who was drumming on an old rusted can. They heard him ask his wife in a low hoarse whisper to bring him his water-pipe, and stood watching him as he inhaled deeply, puffing out the smoke in dense clouds like those which came from damp logs burning in the oven.

When a few men began to go in, they were emboldened to creep in after them. But they were careful to stand near the door watching what was going on with diffidence. Not that anything fearful was going on. Farag, pale and silent, was puffing away quietly, regularly renewing the supply of tobacco, while the men sat round him, embarrassed and self-conscious. When one of them stirred uneasily, feeling compelled to say something to soften the blow, Farag would look at him and quietly offer him a puff from the water-pipe to keep him silent. The thing he had dreaded for a long time had happened at last, and nothing he or anyone else could say was going to make it change.

He remembered how he used to watch his sister's body moving beneath her torn floating black gown, or see her flesh through the holes; how whenever he watched her laugh or speak, or even eat, the blood would race to his head and he would look at her with eyes like hot pokers, or burst into wild laughter by which he hoped to conceal his lurking fear of the impending disaster. Often he had asked himself what he would do if – God forbid – the thing should happen. His hair would stand on end at the thought and he would look at Fatma again and wish he could wipe her off the face of the earth. And now that it had happened it was his duty to act like a man and a brother. It was his duty to kill her and kill Gharib – kill the sister whom he had carried in his arms as a child across the canals, and whom his dying mother had left to his care. It was his duty to kill Gharib, the worthless dog he had sheltered and fed, always half expecting to be betrayed.

Only blood was going to redeem what had happened. But before he made himself guilty of their blood, their own guilt must be proved. He was about to bring ruin on himself and his wife and his children, and it must not be for nothing. Let him smoke then and wait before he took up his knife. The decision was cold and merciless and irrevocable. For Farag was a farm man, and farm people were accused by village folk of being lax in matters of morality. He was going to show them that farm people have a moral code as lofty as their own and that they do not tolerate The Shame.

An enormous black mass with myriad arms and heads was seen coming in the distance, moving in a cloud of dust. It was the women marching resolutely in their ragged black gowns, driving Fatma before them, white as a sheet, the colour gone from her cheeks. There was no trace of beauty now in her face, and her head was covered with her shawl like a woman in mourning as she stared about her, her face a deathlike mask.

They made a lot of noise as they came nearer, arguing in shrill tones. Some said she should be taken to the farm-steward's house while others insisted her place was in her brother's house and that it was more proper for her to be taken there. After a good deal of squabbling she was conducted to the steward's house which stood in a corner of the farm, while the children stopped at the door and waited.

As for Gharib, they said he was last seen heading for the fields. He had run away, perhaps never to return, they said.

Suddenly all was confusion, thoughts were blurred and vision was impaired and no clear course of action seemed open. The men kept silent while the women heaped curses on Gharib, asking God to blight him with a deadly plague. Yet even the women's loud jabbering failed to lift the gloom that was slowly settling on the farm making even the dogs cower quietly in their corners.

Over at the steward's house the ring was closing in on Fatma. She was being badgered with questions, but even before she answered no one was prepared to believe her. She told them she had been taking Farag's breakfast to him in the fields that day, that she was just crossing the canal when Gharib suddenly appeared out of nowhere and tried to grab her by the hand and pull her to him. She fought him and cried out for help. Here she interrupted her rambling account. But the women urged her on. People came to her rescue, she went on, but Gharib had vanished into thin air. They did not believe her. There was more to this. No there wasn't, Fatma insisted. That wasn't true, and they shook their heads and each presented her own interpretation of Gharib's grabbing of Fatma's hand with all the colour her imagination could bring to it. They were seized by a mad fever to know exactly what had happened, which grew increasingly wild and more persistent as Fatma refused to say any more. Even the men sitting round Farag, far from Fatma and her circle, seemed to have caught the same fever although they appeared more restrained.

'Wait and see, folks,' someone would say in kindness, 'perhaps nothing happened.'

No one could ignore any longer what they had tried to suppress, now that it had happened. No one was astonished for it was not difficult to imagine the result when a man found himself alone with Fatma, much less when that man was Gharib. Who was going to believe that she had resisted? If she had indeed been alone with him, all was lost. The important thing now was to find out if all was really lost. Even Farag, as he guessed at the people's secret thoughts, wanted to know the truth not for its own sake but in order to make sure that Fatma was no longer his sister and that he was free to deal with her as he saw fit.

Strangely enough, women are bolder than men when it comes to such matters. They were quick to whisper it first amongst themselves, and then to Farag's wife – who had left the house to go weeping and wailing over Fatma – and then to Fatma's aunt. When they told Fatma herself, her face darkened, her nostrils quivered with anger, and a few tears fell from her eyes, fewer than the drops of juice squeezed out of a green lemon. She screamed at them that she was not going to let them do anything of the kind. She swore on the Koran that she hadn't been touched. 'You're afraid of the examination, so something must have happened,' they all said. All of a sudden she flushed crimson, unable to utter a sound. She who had once

believed it herself, and who had been told by others that
she did not know what it was to be shy.

Had such a thing happened in a village the people would
have done everything to cover up for one of their own.
But on a farm where nothing stays hidden, what was the
use? Everyone, old and young, was on tenterhooks to know
if the inevitable had happened to Fatma as they had
predicted.

The horror of what she was about to face made her grow
faint. They splashed water on her face and put an onion
to her nose to make her come round. Her head reeled at
the thought that she was being accused of the most in-
famous of crimes, that she was entirely at the mercy of
these people, defenceless against their savage prying, within
sight and hearing of her own brother and her relatives
and all those who used to love her and whom she used to
love. She looked up at the circle of women and pleaded for
mercy. They only stared with mournful eyes from which
all doubt had gone. 'Very well,' she said with a stony face,
'I am ready.'

By then Farag's head was in a daze from too much drawing on his water-pipe on an empty stomach. His head was
lowered, resting on his hand. Were he not a man he could
have been taken for a grief-stricken widow bemoaning a
dead husband.

There was no one on the farm more expert on such
matters than Sabha, the *mashtah*,[4] who was not a professional like the others. She owned an old manual sewing
machine and took in sewing for men and women alike. She
looked younger than her years, with a clear complexion
and a good-natured motherly air about her. But when she
spoke she betrayed herself for what she was : a tough,
matter-of-fact woman who had knocked about a good deal,
with much experience of both men and women, and who
did not inspire much confidence.

---

[4] A washer or tire-woman whose profession is to help women with
their toilet, particularly the decking-out of brides on their wedding
day.

When Fatma announced she was ready they should have called in Sabha, but they hesitated. They were keen on having the truth, and although Sabha was experienced in such matters and they were certain that she would know immediately what there was to know, they did not trust her, for she was held in disrepute. True she was the only dressmaker on the farm and she sewed for everybody, but to be seen in her house, even though only to try on a *gallabieh*, was compromising. It was well known that Sabha did not mind herself and her house being used as a screen for the clandestine meetings of men and women who had a perfectly good reason for being there. No one of course had actually seen anything. It might have been true, just as it might have been a groundless rumour, but what was certain was that Sabha was a shady character. She might find out the truth and withhold it, or she might say the opposite of what she knew. 'There's only Om George,' said Farag's wife.

The women agreed immediately. Om George was the only 'lady' on the farm, and the only one who was educated and could read and write. What was more she came from the town, where people knew all about everything.

The children pushed and shoved as they crowded round the long procession leaving the steward's house on its way to the bailiff's. Eager yet dejected, the crowd stumbled on down the narrow lanes littered with dirt and piles of rice straw. It was still daylight although the sun was going down. Fatma, in their midst, walked blindly on, her face ashen, her heart sunk to her feet, feeling with every step that she was trampling on it. Trampling on her innocence, and the sweet memories of her childhood, and the days of her girlhood when she sang at wedding feasts, dreaming of her own wedding day, and the music, and the ritual night when her hands would be dyed with henna – the night when all would stand waiting for her to come out like a queen. And now they were waiting for her too. Hundreds of eyes riveted on her everywhere she looked, ravenous and brutal, raping her without shame as she staggered on, bleeding in her heart, barefooted, humiliated, driven without mercy.

Her friend Hikmat tried to pull her veil down to cover her face but she pushed it back. What was the use of covering her face when all of her was bare?

Sadly, inexorably, the mass of women moved on, heads and arms squirming, a trail of children and hungry dogs behind, all enveloped in a veil of dust. The geese along their path were scared away, and overhead the birds and doves flew to their nests and the women trudged on, grim and resolute, till at last they reached the bailiff's house.

At that moment Dorgham the watchman was having another of his fits, bawling as usual, while nobody paid attention, for people by now were used to his outbursts. He was the only man on the farm who came from Upper Egypt, and he had been watchman to that threshing floor since the day he arrived. He was now well over seventy and still at the same job. He had a huge black head and thick black features constantly knitted into an angry scowl. His hair was kinky and now quite grey, and his long white whiskers made him look like a mastiff. Sweat was constantly pouring from his face so that it glistened as though it were smeared with grease, and he spoke in fierce grunts which nobody understood. The sight of anyone coming near the threshing floor was enough to send him into a rage. After living thirty years on the farm he still did not know anyone by name, nor did he care to, and so long as people stayed away from his threshing floor he left them alone.

Now he was barking at Gharib whom he had discovered hiding under a pile of maize. The boy had just come out of hiding, sneaking back to the farm in order to watch the result of his atrocious act. His already dusky face had browned to a dull tan. He wore his skull-cap low on his forehead, no longer displaying his cherished forelock. It was a much subdued Gharib huddling there beneath the maize, glum and repentant, as his own depravity revealed itself to him in all its starkness. As the procession approached and Fatma appeared he sank deeper in his hiding place and looked away.

It was his dread of Fatma and the fact that she was unattainable that had kindled his desire. And the more desperately he wanted her the more distant she had seemed. He had not intended any harm. All he wanted was a little recognition, a sign that she was aware he existed, if only a careless look over her shoulder. But that never came, and he retaliated by an even more fevered pursuit of other women, never for a moment giving up his passionate longing for one look or one word from Fatma.

That wasn't the first time he had hidden, watching for her as she carried her brother's breakfast to the field, swaying in her black gown, the sweet breath of her body blowing over the trees, and the meadows, and the stream, filling the earth with her fragrance. Many times before he had stood watching for her, unobserved, afraid to be discovered, but that day for the first time he did not care if he was. He wanted her to see him. For the first time he longed to commit that Shame which had kept him sleepless and tormented, tossing on the straw. And yet he would have been content only to speak to that girl who was neither his sister nor his mother and listen to her timid reply.

No sooner had he appeared before her, emerging from the field, than she stood rooted where she was as though she had seen him stark naked. As though it were The Shame itself looming before her. That very Shame of which Farag's bloodshot eyes, branding her like fire, had given her warning. The basket fell off her head. She screamed in panic. Everyone came rushing at the sound. In one second the whole world was tumbling about her ears as Gharib took to his heels and vanished in the fields.

Contrary to what they expected, Om George crossed herself and expressed her genuine sorrow over the whole affair, promising to do her best to help to find out the truth. She swore by the living Christ that she would get her husband to lock up Gharib in the police station, and get the police officer to tie him to the tail of a horse and hang him on a telephone pole. Om George was well known for her piety. She was well-bred and dignified. Nobody knew her real name. She used to force her husband to take her to church in town every Sunday morning in spite of his grumbling. He was used to spending Saturday evenings drinking *arak* in the neighbouring village where Panayoti, the grocer, also served liquor to those who wanted it.

Om George was fair and short with greying hair and three dots tattooed on her chin. She knew all about Fatma, and she was rather fond of the girl. Often she used to send for her to come and help her with the biscuits Abu George[5] couldn't do without for breakfast. Or sometimes just to keep her company, or to fill her in on the latest gossip as she was forbidden to mix with the women of the farm. Had it not been for the difference in age she might have been her best friend.

It was with the deepest humiliation that Fatma stepped into the bailiff's house. She was going there now not because she was wanted, but in order for Om George to arbitrate on her honour; the woman who only a few days before had kissed her mouth saying that had they been of the same religion she would have taken her for wife to her brother who was a cashier in the province of Beheira.

She stood petrified on the threshold but the women dragged her in and her veil slipped off her head. Om George went round to see that George was out of the house and that the doors and panes and shutters were properly barred. Fatma fought with all the strength of instinctive shyness, but they had fallen on her, forcing her down on the bed while one woman tied up her hands and two others got hold of her legs. Many hands stretched towards her : veined, ugly, dry hands. Eyes bulged, intent in their

[5] Father of George.

search for honour, seeking to guard it. Burning, piercing, boring through her, even when they no longer knew what they were looking for. Om George was all in a quiver as though she were the one about to go through the ordeal. She kept rebuking the women, in vain, at the same time reassuring Fatma, also in vain, while the struggle went on amidst muffled cries that gradually died to a chill whisper. A stillness heavy with expectation hung over the room and spread slowly outside, to the house, and onto the farm, and over the whole universe. It hung gloomily over the heads of the people sitting with Farag and those hanging around near the irrigation pump or out in the fields, following in their imaginations what was going on at the bailiff's house.

The whole farm was lulled to a hush except Dorgham. Only one man was there to give him an ear and that was Abdoun, Gharib's father. Lifting his *gallabieh* by the hem he had rushed to the threshing floor in search of any living soul before whom he could vent his fury and curse Fatma and his son and the entire farm – even if only Dorgham.

Suddenly a loud trilling-cry coming from the room where Fatma was imprisoned, tore the silence. It was followed by others, alternating with cries of, 'All is well! Thank God, all is well! Honour is safe.'

Only then did Farag look up. 'Bring her to me,' were the first words he uttered.

A few moments later, no sooner had Dorgham's vociferating died down than a tremendous racket was heard starting near the shaft which fed the old water-wheel. It was deep enough to hold three men standing on one another's shoulders, and there just at the edge was old Abdoun catching his son by the scruff of the neck, and with all his tottering strength trying to throw him in. From all around men had gathered round him in an effort to quell his fury and save Gharib from his clutches. Every time he failed to budge Gharib his vituperations redoubled and his curses poured like burning lava. Anyone watching this performance could have no doubt of Abdoun's genuine intention of drowning his son. But there was something, perhaps an imperceptible inflection in his voice, or in his choice of insults, which suggested that Abdoun was at heart not ashamed of his son. If anything, that he was secretly proud to have sired a seducer no woman could resist, and that his son was accused of rape.

Meanwhile at Farag's house a regular massacre was about to take place. Farag was beating Fatma with the coffee grinder, and Fatma was howling with pain. Farag's wife was screaming in terror lest he should kill his sister and get himself into trouble. The neighbours' wives were screaming too, while everyone else from inside and outside the house rushed to hold him back, in vain. Farag was like a maddened beast heeding nothing but his wild intent to murder his sister. And yet there was something wanting in the measured force of his blows and the look in his eye strangely void of emotion. It was just that although Fatma's innocence was proved, and his honour was untouched, he felt bound to perform some spectacular act by which to reply to the people's gossip and the many speculations that had crossed their minds.

Of course Abdoun never drowned his son, and Farag never murdered his sister. The sun went down as always, and as always people brought their cattle home from the fields, having loaded the donkeys with their fodder. Smoke began to rise through the cracks and over the roof-tops of the mud houses, and cooking smells drifted in the air with the glow of sunset. The men went to evening prayers, and the women finished going up and down to feed the animals and lock the chickens in their coops for the night. By the time the call to the night prayer echoed above the roof-tops, all was quiet on the farm again. Everything concerning the incident had been hashed and rehashed until there was nothing more to add. Heads began to nod, lamps flickered and died. Sleep crept in with the growing darkness and tired bodies stretched on their mats and lay still.

After everyone had gone to sleep and Fatma was alone, weary and broken, she began to cry. Her tears flowed in spite of herself, streaming down onto the mud oven where Farag had forced her to sleep without mat or cover. Her body shook with her sobs, so did the chicken coop by her side, and the oven, and the house, and the entire farm, until she nearly woke the people from their sleep. She gave herself up to her pain and wept far into the night, racked by her suffering.

During the days that followed, well-meaning friends tried to persuade Farag to accept Gharib when he proposed to marry Fatma, but he wouldn't hear of it and they had to give up. As for Gharib, he never talked about Fatma any more. As a matter of fact he stopped talking about women altogether. He cut his forelock and he took to observing the prayers regularly, but that did not prevent him from hanging around the farm, and loitering by the open window of Farag's house.

Fatma, on the other hand, was locked up in the house, forbidden by Farag to step outside or even to go to work although he was in dire need of her earnings. It made no difference, for she had renounced the world, and was quite content with her seclusion. The bloom was gone from her cheeks, and her eyes had lost their lustre. She had grown to look like a sluggish beast : cowering, inert, unsmiling. There was submission in her voice, and her tone had lost the sparkle where her intense femininity rang with every inflection.

Nevertheless none of all this lasted very long. Fatma did not remain a prisoner for ever, and Gharib's zeal for prayer fizzled out, and Farag went back to his boisterous clowning. For after many and many a market day, everything that happened was stowed away in the storehouses of memory. Peacemakers had seen to it that Abdoun was reconciled with his son, and all was well between them. Gharib even grew his forelock again and once more he was entertaining his friends with tales of his amorous exploits. Not without a shade of bitterness. For Fatma was up and about again, ravishing as ever, wearing her headcloth at a slant, holding her gown by the hem, her willowy grace

driving the men out of their senses. She greeted everyone
on her way. Everyone except Gharib; not deliberately, but
simply because she did not see him, as if he had never
existed.

Fatma had returned to her old way of looking and talking and smiling and bewitching the men just as before.
But people wondered sometimes. She had acquired something new, something they did not know her to have
before. Or perhaps one should say she had lost something :
that thing that gave her purity. The quality that gave
sincerity to her smile and made her anger real. She had
lost her innocence. Now she was a creature of guile and
deceit and concealment.

That was not all. If Farag happened to catch her leaving
Sabha's house, and he dragged her home, and locked the
door and grabbing her by the hair asked her what she was
doing there, she could stare him in the face and answer
boldly, 'I was having a fitting. Get out of my way.' And
she would shake herself free of his grip and stand in a
corner of the room rearranging her hair, with her lovely
eyes looking straight at him, defiant, unflinching and un-
abashed.

Because the Day of Judgement Never Comes

He strained once more to listen because what was going on was very important to him. Perhaps the most important thing in his life. There was the neighbours' wireless. They lived wall to wall and it was going full blast. Outside, the children who were still awake were hollering the old rhyme about the bear who had fallen into the well with the pig who was her mate. Had she really fallen, and was she now lying quiet at the bottom of the well? Was her mate a fat corpulent pig like Aboul Seba' Ismail? He very much wanted to hear everything because it was his mother lying up there above him on top of the bed. The mattress was bulging between the boards although his mother was not a fat woman. Why then was the mattress bulging so? But then that was before, when he used to hear only the whispering.

Dinner time, and her shining smile, and the warm rays of her love, and her sleepy voice saying, 'Come on, children, to bed, it's late.' And she would lift the edge of the sheet that hung round the sides of the bed and make them crawl in under it like obedient chickens. Home was only one room. In the summer his favourite place was near the wall because it was cool and he loved to lie near it and rub his naked feet against it. When winter came he moved away from the wall towards the edge. And all year there was this rapping which he could never quite catch because by the time he woke it had stopped and the café would have closed and its bright lights would have been turned off and the whole street would be plunged in darkness.

The door creaked a little when it opened and then he heard
the whispering. Whispering and darkness. That's all there
was. And the rapping, like drops of water dripping onto
the hard surface of the floor. Whispering, like the rustle
of her nightdress. Or perhaps it was the rustle of her nightdress that sounded like whispering. And then his mother
would get into bed. She alone slept on top of the bed,
although it was wide enough to take them all. But she
had insisted on making them sleep below, even when his
father was alive. When they grew up and they grumbled
that their heads knocked against the boards she called in
a carpenter and made him raise the legs to make more
room. As all children would, he loved the cosy shelter of
that nook where he could hide and play. He loved to think
of it as an Arab's tent or a trench, or a holy man's grave.
But all the time there was that craving that made him
long for his mother's arms, long to nestle near her on the
soft mattress and the clean white sheet. Sometimes in the
middle of the night he would feign illness and groan
loudly but he never got any attention except when she'd
had enough of his groans. Then she would ask in a low
voice, full of menace. 'What's wrong, Ibrahim?' and that
would be the end of his groans as they were intended only
to see how far they would get him.

The darkness, and the whispering and then his mother's
wakefulness almost as though it were caused by that
foreign breathing that filled the room from the moment
the door opened. She would toss and turn restlessly on the
bed. One night one of the boards fell down and hit his
sister's leg and she screamed. He screamed too, and when
his mother did not answer immediately he was seized with
panic and went to sleep only after she gave him a smack.
The tossing was surely not from insomnia; surely it was
something else. When did he become aware of that other
thing? Tonight was certainly not the first time. The first
time had been that night before the feast when she had

sent them out of the room so that she could take a bath and they came back and found her drying her hair and her clean nightdress was open and he saw her breasts. That was the first time he realized his mother had breasts. He saw them, and the look in her eye, and he thought he saw a shadow there, as though the world were darkening, and her eyes reminded him of the whispering, and of her breasts. He dared not stay and ran outside to the children yelling about the bear which had fallen into the well. He played for a long time until the dust filled his eyes and he felt drowsy and his head began to go round. Then he returned. He knocked on the door but nobody opened it. Then came his mother's menacing voice. 'Since you're late, you'll sleep on the doorstep.' And she wouldn't let him in that night and he slept outside, which was just what he wanted. But when he woke up in the morning he found himself in his place under the bed, and she was lying near him, his mother. When she saw him waking she gave him a hug and said, 'A happy feast to you, Ibrahim,' and he snuggled up to her feeling the happiest boy in the world. The only thing that bothered him was the scent of her soap. For some reason it was linked with something shameful, something one mustn't do. He took her arm and put it round his neck and he played with her fingers which were darker outside than inside and he kissed her palms and her fingers one by one. It was a long long time since he had last done that for he hadn't slept near her for so long. He felt the warm living flesh of her bosom pressing against him. Her living flesh and the scent of her soap and the peculiar smell of her sweat and the whispering in the dark. They worked him up to the point of tears that fell quietly on her hand. She pulled it away quickly as though she were stung, and when she realized he was crying she hugged him closer and he wanted to run away from her, outside, to the boys yelling about the bear and the pig who was her mate. But when he realized the night was gone, and that the coming day was a feast day when all the other children would be celebrating and getting

presents he burst out crying and didn't stop until his
mother shook him roughly, crying, 'What's the matter,
boy?' Indeed, what was the matter? What had happened?
Nothing. At least nothing to make him cry. Then what
made him so sad? Was it Aboul Seba' sitting there so long,
and the piastre he gave him every time, insisting he must
go and buy himself sweets, even though he didn't want
sweets? He was afraid to go and leave his mother alone
with that man. When he dallied there was his mother's
commanding voice, 'Listen to your uncle Ismail, Borham.'[1]
And Borham would search the man's eyes before he left
the room, looking for some sign that would dispel his fears.
Although he did not fear the man's great bulk or his huge
hand which was the size of his sister's pillow, he could not
keep his eyes on him for long. Something in the man's
shifty look unnerved him. A look where treachery mingled
with irony. The coarse brutish irony of a slovenly oaf who
belched every time he was given a glass of water to drink,
and then went on to talking in his coarse bellow. And when
he leaned over to whisper into his mother's ear his croak
spread like an evil fog and hung about the room and over
their lives with a disturbing sense of shame.

What was it he had against his uncle Aboul Seba' Ismail
in particular? There were many others who came to the
house and shook hands with his mother, and whispered in
her ear, and sometimes they gave him a piastre, and she
laughed and chatted with them all. But when this man
was around he suddenly felt that the invisible tie that
bound him to her no longer existed, that she was no longer
aware he was there, while his own awareness of her would
mount to a frenzy, working him up to a pitch of rage when it
was all he could do to stop himself from poking his father's
cane into her eyes, or suddenly tearing off his clothes to
stand naked just to remind her he was there. Life used to
be easy and sweet and without complications, and he loved
everything in it. He loved their gathering round the table

[1] Borham is a diminutive for Ibrahim.

at mealtimes when he was very hungry, together with his sister and his four-year-old brother who still stuttered when he spoke. He loved the feel of his mother's devotion to them and particularly to himself. And his tea and milk in the morning, and the outings along the river bank, eating lettuce and lupins, and sitting on the grass in the park. How lovely it used to be, even when they talked about his father, and his mother's face clouded and he feared she might cry. They always recalled his virtues. They spoke of him as though he were a saint. They remembered how strong he used to be, almost as if he were Antar ibn Shaddad.[2] And they talked about the malady that carried him off in a week. He died, they said.

Yes. By and by this word which until now had no special significance for him began to acquire meaning. His father had died. That meant he had shut his eyes for ever, and his face had gone pale and cold, and they had wrapped him in a shroud, and they had buried him. He had seen it all but he had understood nothing, just like the rustling and the whispering in the dark, and the people who kept saying after his father died, 'Borham will carry on.' Now the fog was clearing a little and he was able to discern, if nothing very clear, at least vague intimations of something obscure and deep as the mouth of the well where the bear went down with her mate the pig. Even the playing and singing of the children outside left him unmoved that night, although they seemed to be enjoying themselves.

'Well, so you've grown, and filled out like a great big bullock, boy,' said the owner of the Duco workshop where he was employed, as he tweaked his ear. 'So you're no longer a child, boy. Well, I don't like the look of you bending over all day long like that. What's eating you boy, hey? Couldn't be old Tshomba making a bid for you, could it?'

[2] Pre-Islamic hero renowned for his courage.

The implication went home. It stung like a whiplash. 'Don't you say that again, master,' he said, hardly knowing how he dared.

Although he was kicked black and blue for that until his face swelled, he was startled when he heard his master say to his friends later on as they sat smoking their water-pipes, 'What do you say folks, I like that kid; he talked back at me, but I like him. That kid's got guts and he's going to be a lot better than Tshomba.'

Tshomba (derived from Tshombé) was the master's head apprentice. He was older than Ibrahim and darker, with kinky hair and a flat nose and a deep gruff voice, unlike his brother Lomumba. All he did all day was kick Ibrahim around and call him names.

'Remember me to your old woman,' he used to call after him.

The first time Tshomba had said this, Ibrahim flew at him and struck him on the face, but the beating he got in return was such as he would never forget. Surely the first thing he was going to do when he grew up was to kill Tshomba, together with the first bear to come his way. He felt silly now repeating that silly rhyme with the other children. It didn't thrill him any more. And crawling under the bed was a bigger effort now. He found it hard to go to sleep immediately, the moment his head touched the long pillow that had gone flat and stiff as a plank of wood. Now he was able to tell whispering from rustling. He did not wake at the rapping now, but long before it came, when he became attentive to the footsteps in the dark street, and he knew them to be Aboul Seba' Ismail's, and he knew that the café was closing up for the night. He wasn't the only one to become attentive when the bed creaked and his mother's feet stole up and her bracelets clinked. Then the rustling. Then the door opening, and his mother's sleepy whisper, 'Good evening.' She was even the first to greet him. And that croak which no effort could bring to a whisper simply would not make sense. And the man's eyes would catch fire and they looked as if they gave off light making everything in the dark room shine, even his own ugly tawny face, even her naked feet and her toes shrinking under her weight as she climbed up leaving him below with the bed-sheet hanging down all round him. And Yasmin, curled up on herself, drooling innocently as she lay fast asleep. And his little brother stretching at her feet breathing audibly like a man. They're all in the well down there, and the angels are in heaven, and the ceiling of heaven is made of wooden boards through which the mattress bulges, and under the bed everything founders. And the wooden sky threatens to give way. Then the day of judgement will come, and heaven and hell. He'll hang down his head on the day of judgement. And when Tshomba will come to hit him on the head, the loud thundering voice of God will cry from above, 'Keep your hands off!' And the hand will wither. Why doesn't the day of judgement come now and why doesn't the thundering voice cry, 'Keep your hands off!' so that the pig is stricken still, and his mother's voice chokes in her throat forever so that he never hears the whispering again? That whispering that made of her a strange woman with a face he didn't know, a woman he is ashamed of. And when her whispering came muffled and suspicious, her secret, which she should have kept covered like a private part, came out with it. And the more she tried to muffle it the louder it rang so that all their covers and all their blankets could never smother it. Listen. Could this be the voice of the woman who gave birth to him? His mother?

That's right, he remembers now. How could he forget that time when he was Yasmin's age, perhaps younger? He had awakened one night and was about to shout but what he heard made him change his mind. He could hear his father's voice. He was whispering. He was there with his mother on top of the wooden sky and their whispers had ended in laughter which warmed his heart and made him forget his need to urinate and that only a moment ago he had wanted to shout. There was a smack followed

by a playful scuffle, there, on top of the bed. Then a
smothered cry, then again the scuffle which seemed to
have no end. He could not imagine his father whom he
loved and venerated taking part in such a game and when
he remembered his mother was in it too, for some reason
he was so incensed he could have wept except that he
realized it would be foolish. In spite of his resentment the
overwhelming feeling was that he was safe in the warmth
of their nearness, that he was in the game too. He wanted
them to know he was there just the same so he opened his
mouth and bawled. To his surprise the only answer was
renewed laughter, wanton and unrestrained, which made
the bed rock violently. That very same bed where his
mother was lying now, so meek, with nothing of the im-
periousness she showed in the daytime, or the threatening
tone she used when she spoke. Meek and enduring, with
revolting submission, inviting the pig to be more brutal.
His croaking whispers had turned to bellowing like that
of a slaughtered ox. He is no longer a child. Now he knows.
But he does not know everything for there were strange
things going on up there in the sky above his head, near
the brink of the well, which were beyond his understanding.
He could beat them up and come out with the truth, but
he wants things as they are; only voices detached, inco-
herent. Only meekness and brutality, and whispering, and
the threat of the bed-springs collapsing. But still his blood
boils like it boils every time and he keeps breaking into a
sweat. He is unable to stop his brain working, to stop it
from understanding. And then that terrible fear, as though
he had a pair of demons up there above him, openly
defiant, who made love in the evenings, recklessly and without fear. The man's bellow is like a cannibal's and his
mother is an insatiable tigress; her muzzle is still blood-
stained from devouring his little brother; she will have
more. The savagery is mad, unconcealed, like rabid dogs
fighting. And the bedsprings sagging under their weight,
crouching on his chest. And they, and the earth and the
sky, and all the cares of the world lying on top of him,

grinding him slowly, pounding on him, stopping his breath. He can take no more. He will die of madness. Fear of the dawn cripples him so that he cannot scream. Fear keeps him from losing control, throwing everything up, falling on them in his fury with his old brown shoe and smashing their skulls with a hammer. But he knows that no matter how far he is driven he will do no such thing. You've grown, Borham – you've grown to be a great hulk of a bear. Your ear listens, and your eyes pierce the bed-springs like hot pokers, and they see what lies on top. When you were small you did not know. You could only see. Now you see and you know. If only he could obliterate what had happened before and start from the beginning. From tonight, for instance, or tomorrow, as though he had seen or heard nothing before. As though the knowledge were coming to him for the first time and then he would behave according to his reaction. But this will never be because he knows this is not the first time. And before the first time there were blurred and vague perceptions which by and by began to reveal themselves so that when at last full knowledge came it was like stale news; like a distant shadow he recognized long before it came into view.

He did not even dare to make his presence felt. It was different with his father and mother because with them he was safe. But these two were nothing but strangers. A pig and a bear, up there in the sky, on the roof of the world, while he and his brother and his sister are entombed, like their father, down below in that grave with the white sheet hanging round it. Should he cry and appear even in his own eyes like Tshomba's 'plaything' as his master calls him? Should he yell and make a show of himself? He could kill her, even when the stranger goes, but that would destroy whatever was left that kept him close to his mother. For in spite of everything she was still his mother and he was alive because he had a mother, and he could not imagine a life without her. Much less that he should kill her and put an end to her life. He was alive because he had that particular mother. To lose whatever linked them, no matter how frail, was to lose his life. Up there now, with that stranger, she was cut off from him, leaving him in the cold with death in his heart. No one in the world belonged to him, nor he to anyone. Only hope kept him alive. That this passing phase should come to an end and that she would return to him. If he were to cry out, if she were to know that he knew, she would spurn him forever, and the spring from which his life welled would cease to flow, and his mother would cease to be. Only that other woman with the black dress slipped over the transparent silk shift would remain, who sometimes peddled and some-times went as a go-between, toiling to earn their living. Food made him happy not for its own sake but because it came from her toil and her love. And since she toiled for their food it was proof that she loved them. He would rather die than confront her or have her exposed, because his need of her was a thousand times greater than her need of them.

Ever since that man had come into their lives he had the feeling she had no need for them. But her being their mother was the centre upon which their lives were riveted. That was why she must continue to live and he must continue to remain silent. Let her deal with hundreds of men to make a living and support them. Let her talk to him with menace in her voice. Of all the men let her pick that stranger and even be the first to greet him with her husky voice when he came. He will not fight. He will spend long nights listening to those voices coming from the wooden canopy. Voices without laughter, without joy, without the dear and tender tones of his father. Only the grunts of a pig and the panting of a bear that fell into the well. A wide embrace where of her own will she enfolds the corpulent man. And their diabolical and brutish en-counter makes his young being sink deeper and deeper under the bed. And now he had grown. Ever since he was a child he had heard it all, but now it drives him to insanity, and in the last resort he can only follow the wise path and continue to say nothing. And yet the day of judgement will not come, and the thundering voice will not cry, 'Keep your hands off!' and the stranger pig will not be stricken and the woman with the husky voice will not die to let the mother return. A cry reaching out from below the wooden canopy to the sleeping town and the vast earth and the endless vault of heaven. And because the day of judgement will not come he wakes up every morning with despair in his heart and as he leaves the house he steals a look at her and he feels the shaky bond grow weaker, and the mother recedes. Years have passed since his father died and the whispering woman prevails. Forlornly he goes to his work and Tshomba's blows fall on the back of his head. The head of a small dark boy.

'Well, so you've grown and filled out,' says Tshomba, 'like a big fat bear . . . and the bear fell into the well.'

The Freak

Every town in this vast country God gave us has got its own worries. It's got its own people, young and old, male and female, families big and small, Copts and Moslems. A vast universe regulated by laws and also troubled by them. Every once in a while something out of the ordinary appears, like in the case of our town which alone of all others happens to have produced that strange monster which could not be classed as human, nor yet as animal. Neither was he the missing link. A curious creature with no name. Sometimes people called him Sheikh Mohamed, sometimes Sheikha[1] Fatma, but only rarely, to identify him. The fact remained that he was nameless, fatherless and motherless.

Nobody knew where he came from. He was endowed with human features, nevertheless. Two eyes, two ears and a nose, and he walked on two feet, but he still wasn't anywhere near a human being. His neck, for instance, leaned horizontally on one shoulder like the trampled-down stem of a plant. Only one of his eyes was open while the other was shut, and never once did he narrow the one or widen the other. His arms hung limply at his sides like those of a washed *gallabieh* dangling on the line. Short, thick and woolly, his hair was neither that of a man nor of a woman, and his massive build reminded one of a sturdy wall. There was no trace of a beard on his face. His voice might have determined his sex except that he never spoke. He never moved either, unless he was hurt or in pain, in which case he would emit a low whine which was hard to attribute to anything sapient.

[1] Feminine for Sheikh.

He was rarely seen to walk and when he did he shuffled awkwardly in short narrow steps as if his feet were bound. He would post himself in front of one's shop or courtyard and remain standing there for long hours without stirring once. How he fed himself was a mystery, as he never accepted any food that was offered him. Some said he fed on weeds which he picked in the fields, and that he had a liking for clover, and that he drank from the edge of the stream like cattle. But no one could say he had actually seen him do it.

Anywhere else such a creature would have been looked upon as a phenomenon calling for special study, or at least he would have provided the press with a sensational scoop. But in our town nobody looked upon him as someone abnormal, only different. And since he was living peacefully in our midst, doing no harm, no one had a right to mock or molest him. His deformity was a manifestation of God's will which none had a right to contest. His was a vast universe where all had a right to live, the maimed and the crippled and the wise and the insane. All moving in the same slow, fearful procession leading to their end and to infinity.

It was simply that the people regarded The Freak with a special awe which had none of that reverence tinged with irony they reserved for idiots and half-wits. Nor did they feel for him that pity mixed with revulsion which they had for cripples. Perhaps it was the awe inspired by those extraordinary phenomena that reveal the tremendous order of the universe.

When he came upon a gathering, talk continued as usual and no one made him feel his presence was noticed. And when his long stations in one place tempted the children to gather round him and stare, they were reproved and chased all the way back into their warrens, and the punishment for tormenting him was such that they knew better than to try again.

For long years The Freak had lived in our town in this fashion, absolved from every obligation, human or animal.

He could go where he liked, do what he pleased, no one molested him. People allowed him to enter their houses and stay crouching in one of its corners for as long as he wished without his presence disturbing anyone, quite as if he were one of the fixtures. Women undressed before him and so did the men. Private affairs were discussed in his presence, and men made love to their wives or other people's under his eye. Conspiracies were planned and false accusations plotted while he looked on. Anyone hesitating about speaking his mind or divulging a secret was quickly assured, 'You may speak without fear, there's only you and I and The Freak.'

Nevertheless, every few years a rumour would spread concerning him. They said there was something between him and Hobble-Foot Na'asa, for she had often been seen to seek him by night. She was often seen, also by night, leaving the vacant lot by the mosque where he slept. Surely they were lovers. Another rumour had it he was the illegitimate child she bore by a man of degenerate blood from the central town where she used to go at dawn selling cheese and milk and loads of wood.

Both rumours were found to be far-fetched as Na'asa hardly counted as a female. She was hard, and flat, and bony, like a man. If she got involved in a brawl she was sure to emerge without a scratch, leaving behind several wounded men to her credit.

She had been widowed when still very young and had had to struggle for her living ever since, doing the ordinary jobs allotted to women. But she was more like a man in disposition, which is perhaps why she did not remarry and why she fell to doing the work for which her muscular build adapted her. She carried loads of wood and hay and meal. Her only equipment was a thick round disk, which she had sewn for herself from old rags, which formed a rest she placed on her head, and on that she could sit a camel's load. She walked erect, striding powerfully, her feet beating the ground, her anklets, perhaps the only indication of her femininity, clinking as they knocked against each other. Except that being so used to loads, when she walked without them, she was bound to lose her balance and skip along like a grasshopper, now with the gait of a female, now with the stomp of a male, which made people nickname her Hobble-Foot. The men out of jealousy, the women in contempt. Both were unfair. A woman so unfeminine could hardly be connected with a love affair, nor was it conceivable that she could mother a child, even if it were only a monster like The Freak.

But rumour was strong in spite of that. After she gave birth, they said, she hid him in that same vacant lot where he lodged now, feeding him on the quiet, letting him out only when he grew. One year when there was much talk about lewd women, the story went that the starved and the lustful from the edge of town went to him for solace, confident of his silence, knowing his tongue would never wag. Another story alleged he was born of an ape. A woman, weary of her sterility, had gone to a gipsy who prescribed the wool remedy. As bad luck would have it the rag happened to contain the sperm of an ape which made her conceive and give birth to The Freak. Horrified at the sight of the creature the woman gave him to the gipsy with money to keep her mouth shut and bring him up. The gipsy took him away with her on her many wanderings and, returning after he had grown, abandoned him just outside the town.

The following year another story went round insinuating that The Freak was only the son of Abdou El Bitar who went round shaving donkeys and trimming their hooves and who, it was said, and God only knew, had a predilection for the females of the species. Sheikh El Beledi's in particular, and that it was the latter who got rid of the new-born infant for fear of its being foisted on him, or possibly his son who, they say, was also given to the same vice.

Rumours and stories, remote, sly, inconsistent, but continuous, proved the people's determination to uncover the truth.

He could have gone on living like that in our town for ever, being and not being, existing and not existing, if one night one of the El Abayda boys hadn't come running in a fright. He threw himself down, panting and trembling all over, before the crowd which usually sat up at night in the lane near the mill.

'What's come over you?'

'Well, what do you think, folks? It's The Freak. He can speak as good as you and I put together,' he said, stuttering like all the rest of his family.

'It can't be, boy, how do you know?'

He swore on his father's grave that he had been passing by the vacant lot when he heard two people talking in low voices. He drew nearer and discovered it was Hobble-Foot Na'asa talking to The Freak who was answering in a perfectly normal voice, every word perfectly clear. He couldn't believe his ears and he drew nearer still, but when Na'asa saw him she barked at him and he ran away in terror to come and tell them.

No one believed him. They all agreed the boy was ranting. The vacant lot had terrified him for some reason and his imagination was playing tricks on him. Very likely it was the djinn he had heard talking. That was easier to believe than that The Freak could speak. Was it possible he had fooled them all those years, and what did he stand to gain by that? Tormenting himself standing motionless for long hours, sleeping like an animal, living like vermin.

Yet, in spite of their powerful arguments and their absolute refusal to believe what the boy had said, doubt began to set in. There was a hint of distrust in their look now when they saw him hanging around his usual haunts. What if it were true? What if all along The Freak could see and hear and understand? It was a frightful thought. All those years he had been looked upon as a non-existent being. He had been allowed to see and hear what no other had seen or heard because he did not count. Something like a domestic animal. A cat or a dog. If household pets were to speak of the things they hear and see few people could go on living. For a man to live as an individual he needs clothing to protect his body and cover his secrets. And in order to exist in a group he must hedge in a portion of himself. That portion where his secret being lies, which sets him apart from others and makes him independent. Just like a family needs the solid walls of a house to preserve its entity, and a town needs a boundary to protect itself from disintegration.

If the news were true, it would be a disaster. It might not yet mean the crumbling of the protecting walls, but it would be the start of a fissure from which all that is contained within would leak outside and then all hell would break loose.

From now on The Freak came to be regarded with fear and suspicion while he remained unchanged, his neck bent and twisted, his blue *gallabieh* dirty and in rags. Sitting or standing he still remained motionless with one eye still shut, the other half open, his face an expressionless mask. Even when suspicion drove the people to hover round him, probing, questioning, trying to pierce his enigmatic exterior, not a nerve twitched, not a muscle moved in that solid mass of flesh.

It was some time before the scare which the news had raised began to calm down. The wave of fear that swept them at the thought that a prying eye had reached into the hidden corners was slowly subsiding, and whatever misgivings there were began to melt away.

The incident could well have been forgotten like the rumours, had not another one occurred which was reported this time not by a frightened boy but by grown men who swore to what they had seen.

It was there, at El Sa'adani's shed tucked under the bridge where he brewed tea and coffee for those who stopped by, that it happened. They were all still discussing the story told by the El Abayda boy. The Freak had chosen to plant himself in a spot of sunshine on top of the bridge, and his face was pouring with sweat. Their talk, sly and full of malice, had come round to Hobble-Foot Na'asa, reporting hearsay and mere rumours as facts, each trying to outdo the other for a sensation until one of them swore she had seduced him. All of a sudden a piercing cry cut through the air; something between a bellow and a roar followed by a deep moan. Even more strange was the voice crying 'God forbid' according to some, 'or God damn you!' according to others. What they all agreed upon was that it was a human voice distinctly coming from somewhere in their vicinity. When they turned to look for its source, they saw The Freak walking in a hurry, leaving his place in the sun and disappearing quickly into the maize field. A day or two later, even though they all agreed that what they saw and heard was beyond doubt, if questioned further they now wouldn't swear. 'God only knows,' they would say, 'but if it wasn't him who could it be? The bridge?'

The town was agog with controversy, a large part of it insisting they had been duped by The Freak. All those years he had been shamming in order to be in on their secrets and to pry into their private affairs. The rest of them stuck to their conviction that the bridge was more likely to speak than that The Freak should utter a human sound.

However, their polemics were only on the surface, for in their hearts clouds of fear were massing. When they reviewed the things they had allowed The Freak to witness their fear turned to horror. They started to comb the town searching for him in the hope that the sight of his monstrous form might calm their fears and confirm their belief that he had no link with humanity. But The Freak was nowhere to be found, which only increased their apprehension. For where could he be, and who could he be talking to?

It was not long before he appeared again, one day, returning from the central town. Na'asa was leading him by the hand. No sooner had news of his return spread than the entire village went out to meet him. The women especially, a huge black lump stuck on the compact block of human beings which had formed around him and Na'asa, were in a towering rage, largely induced by fear. They looked at the pair with eyes darting fire. Nothing had changed in The Freak. The same blue shapeless garment, the same bristling hair. Perhaps his slanting neck was a little less slanting. But the strange thing was the snigger with which he answered when he was addressed. A snigger nearer to speech than to a chuckle.

For a long time Na'asa would not speak, eyeing the crowd in silence. Then suddenly, unable to contain herself any longer, she burst into a volley of abuse, asking why they were collected there, cursing the lot from the oldest to the youngest.

'Alright, you filthy lot of bastards. What do you want? What business is it of yours whether or not he is my son? Whether or not he is dumb? What do you want with him? Alright, so he was sick and I took care of him, is that a crime? Or supposing even he never was sick, that all the time he heard and he saw, what are you afraid of? None of you is any less rotten than his neighbour. Get out of my way, I tell you, or by God I swear if I lay my hands on one of you, I won't let go until I've choked the life out of him.'

They stood listening in amazement, tongue-tied before that sudden outburst. She had ripped off every vestige of shame, was willing to admit The Freak was her son, was ready to reveal his father's name if she had to, while they all stood about speechless, unable to withstand the torrent that was tumbling about their ears.

But sooner or later they were bound to disperse. Sooner or later the morrow had to come. The Freak began to roam about again, stopping here and there where he was wont to stop. Only now wherever he appeared conversation stood still if only for a moment and all eyes would be on him. They were met with the new snigger which only rekindled their fears. What was the wretch sniggering

about? Could it be about the measure of wheat stolen
from the threshing floor while he had stood looking on?
Or because he knew the secret of the bloodstain clinging
to the hem of the *gallabieh*, or about yesterday's cant in
the presence of other company?

When the next day came, and the next one, and the
next, it became clear that their worst fears were confirmed.
The Freak's idiotic snigger was the fissure in the inner
walls through which all that lay hidden threatened to run
out. They realized that in his presence they were stripped
of all covering. They realized they could not live in the
shadow of one before whom they were naked to the bone,
taunted by his evil laugh everywhere they went.

So it was inevitable for the people to wake up horrified
one morning to the sound of a long screaming howl torn
from the depths of an anguished heart. 'Oh, my son! Oh,
my beloved!' it wailed again and again. They all rushed out
in its direction. It was coming from the vacant lot. There,
they found Na'asa. When she saw them come near she
started to hurl stones at them. She cursed and wept bitterly,
saying he had always been deaf and dumb, warning them
savagely of her revenge. At her feet lay The Freak in a
pool of blood, his head bashed in by a stone.